Less Than A Week

By: Lauren Lodico

DEDICATION:

This story is dedicated to all the teenagers out there who feel alone, who feel like there is nothing left. You have your whole life ahead of you, just hold on a little longer. There is a beautiful light at the end of the tunnel.

PROLOGUE:

I never expected any of this to happen to a caged-in girl like me. I guess it was the way he looked. Or maybe it was the way he made me feel. Even after all this time spent getting over it – over him – I still don't know.. I guess you could say he made me feel different than anybody else ever had. No wait, that's cheesy. Ugh, he was just special and he made me feel special whenever I was around him.

Now, even after listening to all those heartbreak songs and eating the last container of vanilla ice cream in my house, I can't help grinning every time I think of him. So what if we broke up? We still made amazing memories when we were together. I wouldn't declare him a horrible guy, but I never said I liked him anymore either. He reached deep into my chest and ripped my heart away from the rest of my organs. He took something that never belonged to him in the first place and he ruined it. And I would never forgive him for that. I can't quite figure out why we even broke up.

It could've been something in the air that made us drift away. It could've been anything really, but that's not why I'm doing this. Today is the first day since the break-up that I have gotten up, after spending a week sitting on the couch and feeling bad for myself. After countless hours of watching re-runs of "I Love Lucy," I had an epiphany.

Heartbreak has to be the number one cause of tears in the world. How could I save people from everything I went through? How could I help girls like me who were going through relationships and troubles with friends and boys? How could I help a girl going through heartbreak? I decided that by writing a blog, girls could get advice from me that they couldn't get from their teachers or from their parents. Just because parents say they know what you are going though doesn't exactly mean they've been through the same exact thing in their childhood. Times have changed and feelings have altered.

So I'm going to start writing once a week, or twice on a good week. I hope to help many who have problems with their social lives. I haven't come up with a good name for the forum yet so if you have any ideas, feel free to message me on my account. I hope that I can help some people out there who are lost when it comes to boys, relationships, friends, and heartbreaks.

Each week I will probably post a new topic, depending on what happens during the week to me. Hope this helps.

XOXO,

Lorraine.

****

A couple hours later....

INCOMING MESSAGE FROM KITTY1242:

Hey Lorraine. My name is Kitty and I have recently read ur first blog post abt your new forum. I had an idea for a name and I thought u might want to know. Well, here it is:

"A Guide to Heartbreak and Other Misfortunes."

Hope u like it. I'll be reading each week; thanks for doing this. I've had a lot of troubles lately and I think hearing advice will solve so many things that would have driven me insane. Anyways, I understand that you're busy so thanks for helping people like me.

KITTY1242

REPLY:

Your welcome, Kitty1242. Thank you so much for the awesome name and I hope that someday, I can meet my first fan in public.

XOXO,

Lorraine.

UPDATED FORUM NAME:

A Guide to Heartbreak and Other Misfortunes.

YOUR FORUM NAME HAS BEEN SAVED.

****

My mind races about Lucas, my mom, my dad, and John as I'm driving to school, 25 miles per hour being minuscule to my over-100-miles per hour thoughts. They pressed me forward, pushing on my body and then all of a sudden, without my knowledge, things found themselves at a halt, a stop sign with red flashing lights and an ambulance. But I continued to move forward towards school.

Eventually, life rushes at you, frontward or backward, it's never really explained what's going to be staring you in the face at the next turn. But my mind stops as I roll backwards and every worry I have slowly becomes negligible. I felt everything just stop but then, it was as if nothing ever happened; everything sped up again.

****

CHAPTER 1:

FIRST DAY GOING BACK TO SCHOOL SINCE THE HEARTBREAK:

I don't know why I am going back. Maybe it is because I feel bad that my mother and brother saw me weak and couldn't do anything about it, or maybe it was because I was trying to go back for myself, trying to fix myself. I need be my own anchor because my old anchor had weighed the ship down far too much. The biggest reason I am probably going back to school has to be because of, "A Guide to Heartbreak and Other Misfortunes." I need to write for the forum. Therefore, I need to experience all that a girl doesn't want to experience.

As I walk in late, heads turn, people whisper, and gasps come from left and right as people realize he isn't walking down the halls with me anymore. I guess you could infer that by us not walking down the halls anymore, we broke up. And just by looking at me, you can tell it was a hard break-up. My hair is tied back in a messy bun when it used to be out and flowing like the wind. My makeup is all gone, because I didn't feel like looking good this morning, and my face looks like I got hit by a bright yellow bus on its way to drop young children off to school. I have bags under my eyes, light and barely noticeable cuts going down my face from my nails, and my lips are swollen and purple from the cold weather outside. I can feel the stares as I go straight to class.

Class can't be more boring. It's third period and I already want to write on my blog instead of sitting next to my best friend. She's been on my case ever since the break-up. She wants to know what happened and tell the whole school because my best friend is the gossip of the school. My phone was ringing so much that I had turned my phone off, something I never do.

Katherine and I have been friends ever since kindergarten. When we got to high school, she changed. She became like every other caked-face, tight clothed, over-the-top attitude teenage girl that surrounds our nation. And I hate that about her.

That's what makes me stand out from the entire school. I am myself and they are all hiding behind a façade. Though I stand by myself, people still feel the need to talk about me as if I have done something wrong to them. I can hear the voices when they talk about me throughout the day. I can feel the noise and sometimes it pierces my shield but other times, it just bounces off me like a trampoline.

"So what exactly happened, Lor?" Katherine whispers to me, turning her head around while our teacher continues to carve his piece of chalk into the black abyss of the board.

"Would you just leave me alone right now, Katherine? I can't put up with your bullshit right now." I don't make eye contact with my best friend, whose eyes, in an instant, portray a broken heart just like mine. Her hazelnut eyes look as if they are pierced by a dagger.

"W-Wh-at?" She's slightly taken back by my sudden harsh behavior. Then again, she should've expected it from me because of what happened.

"You know what I said, Katherine. I'm not repeating myself just for effect or to cause a scene." I don't care at this point. Our relationship has been ruined ever since she became the gossip and I became the old fashioned girl who decided to be herself and nobody else. I stop caring for everything at this moment. My heart is broken and all the love I had left has poured out. Katherine turned around to face the blackboard, tears burning in her eyes. The bell rang, and I quickly made my way out of the classroom, where I lost someone who was once my best friend.

****

Seconds seem like years, minutes seem like decades, and hours seem like centuries. Passing faces remind me of some memories and the places I've been. I wouldn't be the same person; I couldn't be the same person I used to be. In the past, I'd been too forgiving and I'd let people in that I shouldn't have. My biggest mistake was thinking Lucas was different from every other guy.

Lucas James Kelly.

As Lucas walks by, all eyes are on him and whatever girl that is stupid enough to think that he wanted her; she clings to his bicep just like I used to. How I wish I hated Lucas James Kelly for breaking my heart, for making me lost, and for letting me love him so much it hurts. And as his eyes gaze upon me for a split second, I feel my heart beat out of my chest and into his hands once again. I stare at him with a confusing mix of love, passion, and hatred. And just as I pull my stare back and walk away, Lucas comes running. He leaves his newly found girlfriend and comes to me. At first, I hope he's going to talk to me, but then I realize that he's not mine anymore.

"Lorri." He calls out, making my eyes shut tight with fresh tears. He can't see me cry. I think the world is ending as he calls me by my special nickname; the one he gave me on our first date.

"I was surprised when you wanted to go out with me, Luke." I smile, looking up at the sweetheart that was Lucas Kelly, my date.

"Anybody would want to go out with you, Lorri." He eyes me with pride before holding the door open for me as we walked inside my favorite restaurant.

The name sort of stuck afterwards.

"Lorri, would you just listen to me for a second?" He pleas, grabbing my arm as I keep walking. I stop in my tracks and turn around, facing the boy who broke my heart.

"What would Lucas James Kelly possibly want to say to me after breaking my heart with not even so much as a reason?" My eyes shut tightly.

"Open your eyes." He grazes my eyelids with his soft fingertips, making two tears silently run down my face. Lucas wipes them away as quick as they run.

"Stop doing this to me." I look at the back of his impatient girlfriend, who is walking off to class behind him. If it were me, I would've—I can't do this.

"I just want to talk to you, Lorri. I don't want to—"

"You don't have control over my decisions anymore. You cannot have anything you want from me. And I know you don't hear the word no often but here it is: no! Whatever you want from me, you can't have." I rush out of that school and into the parking lot, not caring if the school called my mother or gave me detention.

"Lorri, would you stop running?" Lucas calls out from behind me as I make my way towards my deep blue car.

"Leave me alone, Lucas. You broke my heart once, stop trying to do it again." I fumble for the keys inside my bag.

"Let me explain. I'm sorry." He pants while standing face-to-face with me.

"You don't get to explain or be sorry!" I scream, pushing him back with the strength I could muster from deep within.

"You don't get to do this to me." I sob, taking the key from my hands and opening the car door before he could say anything else. I started the car and would have driven off but Lucas decided to take matters into his own hands and opens the driver's seat of my car.

"What the hell are you doing?" I ask, puzzled, my vision unclear from the tears that were involuntarily streaming down my face.

"I'm taking you home." He demands before lifting me out of the driver's seat, thinking that he could do something heroic again.

"Get the hell off of me." I shove before jumping out of his arms and telling him, "You don't get to be a hero in my life anymore. I don't even want you in my life anymore."

I get into the car and leave without another word to Lucas James Kelly, my ex-everything.

****

"Honey, what are you doing home?" My mother questions me as she looks at my hunched shoulders.

"I couldn't handle—Lucas tried talking to me." I peel off my hoodie, showing my pale face and my reddened eyes.

"Oh, honey." My mother says, saddened even more by the topic, wrapping her arms around me like a blanket. She too liked Lucas, along with my father who could've been in love with Lucas. But my little brother completely admitted to being in love with Lucas.

When I told Johnny that Lucas broke up with me, I think he cried more than me. Lucas used to come over occasionally just to take Johnny to the park for a bit. My father was rarely around to play with Johnny and, when he was around, he would sleep most of the time. Which is why my mom was always the way she was; lonely, depressed, anxious, scared of everything, and sometimes, she would just randomly blackout and sweat uncontrollably.

"Things will get better, I promise. See when you love someone—"

"I didn't love him, Mom." I release my grip on her back and climbing up the stairs to my room, where I get ready to type away on my laptop for the forum.

"LORRAINE." My mother bursts like a bubble. She always did this, just so I could come down and fight her own battles for her but she needed to start defending herself on her own. I could barely handle my own battles, never mind fight other people's.

As soon as I get ready to write, I know I won't be able. There is some type of block in my mind and I can't release its hold. I try relaxing with music and putting my head down but nothing seems to bring the words to my mind to describe today for the readers on my forum, or for *KITTY1242*. So I grab my jacket, leave the house, and drive over to Billy's Bar with my computer opposite of me in the passenger seat.

After receiving my latte and setting up my computer, I open the forum and try to write again; this time, with more luck than last time. But still not enough to describe my day and its misfortunes. I groan and place my head in my hands, frustrated.

"Are you okay?" A stranger softly asks as I lift my head to look at the mysterious voice.

A guy stood in front of me, looking around my age with an apron and hat on that reads, *"Billy's Bar."*

"I'm fine. I just can't seem to find the words to write." I offer him a small smile.

"Do you mind?" He gestures towards the seat that was opposite of me in the corner booth.

"Not at all." I comment, smirking at this cute boy who sat in front of me.

"If you don't mind me asking, what are you writing for?" He puts his rag down on the table and folds his hands.

"Well, I started this blog because—"

And just like that, I talk to this stranger, without crying and tell him about Lucas and my forum.

"I think it's good that you're doing this. Maybe it'll help heal you while providing information for other people out there." He plays around with his rag.

"I've told you pretty much everything about me. Tell me something about you." I say before he stands up.

"Maybe after I get off of work; I'm pretty sure sitting down and talking with a customer could get me fired." He laughs and walks towards the counter.

"Then, why did you do it?"

"It looked like you could use someone to talk to." He shrugs, giving me a smile before serving a customer in line. I turn around and a smile forms on my face from that stranger's consideration and exuberance; his good intentions and humanity got my fingers to type and my mind to form sentences. As I sat there typing away, the sky outside started to change color. The later I stayed at Billy's, the more words appeared on my computer screen.

"Lorraine, we are closing soon." The stranger who had been so generous as to sit down and risk his job, just to help provide me with good conversation and some understanding to break my writer's block, touched my shoulder to warn me of the bar closing.

"How did you know my name?" I ask, suspiciously.

"You end your messages with, '*XOXO Lorraine*." He laughs at my apprehensiveness.

"How did you even know that?" I ask him quickly, being cautious.

"You told me the name of your blog so while I was on break, I looked it up and I may have started following it." He says looking at me as if I was absurd.

"Oh," I giggle nervously.

"Anyway, you wanted to know something about me. I'm closing up so if you'd give me five minutes—" He smiles casually.

"Sure." I return my focus back to the computer.

I go back to typing and getting lost in my own words, some making me feel a deep and dark emotion but others giving me hope that the world isn't such a crepuscular place after all. And as the sky becomes a vague dusk, the gigantic paragraph on my computer screen grows larger and larger.

"So, I guess I have to tell you something about me." The boy sits down across from me, throwing his feet up on another chair while threading his hands together and placing them behind his head to support it.

"I guess you do." I look amused.

"Well, for starters, my name is Cooper." He looks delighted to be sitting across from me.

"Okay, Cooper. How old are you?" I inquire.

"Seventeen but I'll be eighteen in a couple of months." He grins from ear to ear.

"Wow. How does that feel?" I ask him with a smile plastered on my face. I am only sixteen but my birthday is tomorrow. I decide not to tell Cooper this because I don't make a big stink over my birthday anymore. It's just another day for me.

"Good, I guess. I don't know. College is coming soon and it looks like if I want to go, I'm going to have to get a scholarship. My dad can barely pay for us to survive now, you know? And my mom, well, she left us when I was small."

"I'm sorry." I sincerely say but in the back of my mind, I wonder how he could share such salient details with me.

"It's okay. I barely knew her. It doesn't hurt me as much as it hurts my dad." He shrugs.

"What do you want to go to college for?" I ask him, curiously, changing the subject.

"I've always wanted to be an art teacher or maybe like an artist, but I don't think that I'll be able to go to college for it because specialized schools have gigantic bills." He stands from the booth, the rag located in his hands once again.

"Listen, if you want something, go after it. Even if it costs a lot. Who knows? Maybe a miracle will happen and you'll be able to go to any college you want." I try to encourage a soul who has the passion but needs the motivation.

"Yeah but what if I'm not good enough, you know?" He cleans the counter. I walk up to the counter and take the rag from him.

"Whatever your passion is, work at it and you will become great. In fact, I want you to draw me. Since you want to be an art major, you should be able to draw me." I've always wanted someone to draw me from their point of view, I thought, smiling.

"It might take me a couple of days." He leans against the counter and stares into my crystallized blue eyes.

"I can wait."

"Where do you go to school?" He tilts his head against his palm.

"Bay Ville High." I blush and look away.

Everyone knew Bay Ville was the sophisticated school to put your children in, but for me, it was home. Our rivals, Lakewood High, Home of the Lions, is the more troubled school where most parents threw their children.

"Home of the Bears." Cooper nods.

"You go to Lakewood, don't you?" I put a hand against my head in embarrassment.

"I do. But I'm not judging you for going to Bay Ville. I don't care honestly." He puts his hands up in surrender.

"How are you doing with the writing?" He inclines his head towards the computer that was on the table.

"I wrote a lot about today. I just don't know if it's enough *about* today. You know? A lot of things happened today and I just want to make sure I covered everything." I explain to Cooper, whose last name I didn't even know. Yet, I am confiding in him information I barely share with my true friends; true friends that don't really exist.

"I get it," He nods in understanding.

"I don't even know why I am talking to you. I don't even know your last name!" I laugh lightly.

"Ross." He quirks as I feel his eyes on me.

"Cooper Ross?" I ask him, making sure I heard him right.

"Cooper *Allen* Ross." His lips form a smirk.

"CAR?" I chuckle.

"Yep, laugh it up all you want. As long as it's not tears of sadness I'm dealing with." He goes back to work with his discolored rag.

"Okay, okay. I'm sorry. But it's a cool name." I offer, trying to make up for laughing at him.

"You help me clean up and I'll help you edit your writing. Deal?" He suggests to me, continuing to wipe down the counter before moving to wipe down the machines behind him.

"Deal." I roll up my sleeves and get to work by cleaning off the tables.

After a couple of minutes in silence, I get exhausted from sound of chaotic winds outside and put music on from my computer.

"We Don't Have to Take Our Clothes Off," by Ella Eyre, originally by Jermaine Stewart was first to play out of my low speakers.

"Is this okay with you?"

"It's perfect actually. I like this song." He confirms, going back to cleaning. I hang all the chairs up on the tables when they were clean. Cooper takes a mop and wipes the floors quickly.

"I should get a job here now." I chime at Cooper before sitting down at the booth where I had been working. All the cleaning was done and Cooper had promised to edit my next writing before I posted it. As Cooper scanned his eyes all over my writing, I watched his facial reactions with worry in my eyes. I fret because what if he liked it or if he wanted to change everything because it was bad?

As he turned the computer back over to me, he doesn't say a word or show any emotion on his face. He just raises up out of his seat, takes my hand, and pulls me into his arms. His strong-smelling cologne that smells like ocean tides burns my nose and reminds me of Lucas's soft-smelling scent. Tears burn in my eyes and I smile through the pain, uttering, "You know, Lucas would never do this for me."

"Lucas is an asshole; you deserve way better than that." Cooper juts, making me feel better and worse. Part of me still loves Lucas for the guy that he was when we were together but part of me hates him for pushing me away with no reason at all, or with a reason I didn't know about.

"It's okay. I'm fine." I sigh, wiping at the stupid tears that fell from my face, uncontrollably.

"No, it's not. You don't have to bullshit me, Lorraine." Cooper addresses, pushing my head against his chest. The warmth that his chest provided made my eyes heavy and my mind vacant. Sleep pours over my body like the rain that poured from the skies outside. I exit Cooper's safe arms and close my computer, packing it away in my bag.

"I think I'm going to head home. Thank you for today." I sniffle, giving him a small half-hug before exiting Billy's Bar that had always held a piece of my heart. Now, it held a healed piece of it.

"Wait, Lorraine!" Cooper shouts out, following me into the pouring rain, his head of hair clinging to his scalp due to the water coming down from the clouds.

I turn around to face Cooper after throwing my bag into the car so that it doesn't get drenched.

"I know that you may not think it, but you are beautiful *even* when you are sad." He kisses my forehead before encasing my body in his arms. The warmth was still there, even though we were in the cold, soaking in water from the skies. He is a stranger, but he is my stranger for some odd reason.

"What was that for?"

"Because you deserve more than anything anybody can offer you." His cheek brushing mine, trying to get to my ear. I kiss his cheek, smiling.

"What was that for?" It was his turn to question me.

"Because you deserve more than anything anybody can offer you. Plus, I have no idea if I am ever going to see you again." I smile at him.

"We'll see each other again. I promise." I thank him one more time before getting in my car and driving away from Billy's, the place where I met Cooper Allen Ross, CAR; a stranger whom I never thought would show me as much kindness as he did.

****

When I walk in the door at home, I wonder if I will ever see Cooper again. Cooper Allen Ross isn't a person I could ever forget. His kindness and compassion showed me how to be considerate and well-mannered again. His bravery to just put his job on the line to heal a soul, fixed my heart the slightest bit so I could keep pushing forward.

"Where have you been?" This is the first thing that my mother badgers me with as I walk into my front door with a slam. She has an agitated expression on her face with a glass of something in her hand, and I am pretty sure I don't need to look in the glass to figure out the substance that was swirling inside.

"I went out for a bit. Why, Mom?" A distinct expression frozen on my face.

"Lucas stopped by; he wanted to make sure you got home okay." My mom slurs, not caring but telling me just to make it seem like she cared. I knew she was having an anxiety attack right now because of the way her hands were shaking. Helping her though, that was out of my comfort zone for right now.

"What did you tell him?" I am not really processing what is happening because part of me is still stuck on Cooper Allen Ross and his funny initials.

"I told him that you went out. He said he would check on you later. But he never came by again." She gets up from her position at the table to stand in front of me.

I nod, without another word to my mother about a boy, who had broken my heart while my mind was stuck on the boy who healed it the slightest bit.

"Where did you go?" She demands, clearly unworthy of that answer, staring at my eyes with such a brutal love, a love that I despise.

"Out." I infuriate her more by saying so before walking up the stairs with my bag around my shoulder into my room where I shut the door. Leaning against the back of it, I release a deep breath I had no idea I had been holding in. Before jumping into the shower and cleansing my body of the smell of Cooper and the rain, I place my computer on the desk and set it up for when I come out. I change into comfortable pants and a long t-shirt after showering.

"Okay." I huff before opening, '*A Guide to Heartbreak and Other Misfortunes.*'

My entry is open and as I read through it, I remember all of today's emotions that would be erased as soon as my head hit the pillow. I type a bit more after deciding to add Cooper Allen Ross because he healed a piece of me that I couldn't have healed myself.

After writing for what felt like hours on top of hours, I read the full entry and decide that it is well enough to post. Posting it makes me feel accomplished and relieved for some reason. I think that the blog is helping me heal in a way because it's making me feel important and needed. I get two messages a couple of minutes after posting it.

2 INCOMING MESSAGES:

•KITTY1242

•ANN1295

I open KITTY1242's message first because I had already talked to Kitty and she had given me the blog title.

MESSAGE FROM KITTY1242:

Hi, Lorraine. I just wanted to tell you that I'm sorry about your best friend. She probably really cares about you still though. And she probably changed because she had to. Sometimes people get sick of who they are and a change in their life is what they need. I know because I have the same lifestyle as your ex-friend. Maybe she was just trying to help you this time.

My friend was going through the same thing you are going through right now and she turned away from me. I wish I could go back and do something about it but I can't. If you don't heal your friendship, it'll die and along with it, you'll gain regret for not fixing something that could've lasted with you through your entire life. Fix your relationship with your best friend. She needs you just as much as you need her now.

KITTY1242

REPLY:

Hi, Kitty. You have made me think about my once best friend and I think that in a way you are right but if you don't mind me saying so, you don't know my ex-friend. She is the gossip of the school and I don't remember a time, when we were in high school that she was there for me. Why should I be there for someone who isn't there for me?

Thank you for your concern over my relationship with her and the side effects but I don't think that I will suffer consequences of losing someone who hadn't mattered to me since I graduated 8th grade. I'm sorry that you had to recall your memories when the same happened to you but it looks like we are heading down the same road because my old best friend is not a person who deserves any more of my time.

XOXO,

Lorraine.

MESSAGE FROM ANN1295:

Hi, Lorraine. My name is Ann and I am a mother of a teenager. I think that it would be wise to talk to your mother about everything that you are going through instead of writing it on a forum. But I do think that this is a wonderful idea to let other teens know about your experiences so that they are informed about what being a teenager is really like; heartbreak, and many other misfortunes as it says in your title.

If you have a mother present or even a father figure at home, I think it would be a good choice to talk to them about all of your problems and "misfortunes" in life. As a mother myself, I know that if my teenager was going through this, I would want her to turn to me as friend and mother for advice. I suggest doing the same. Who knows? Maybe your mother or father has been through something vaguely the same.

Yours Truly,

ANN1295

REPLY TO ANN1295:

Ann, I hate to tell you but my mother is different. She doesn't know everything that has happened in my relationships because I don't really like talking to my mother. It's better to talk to a stranger because you don't know if you are ever going to see them again. Talking to my mother is a hard thing to do because I have never been extremely close with her. She is not someone that is the easiest to get close to. I have tried to talk to her when I was little but she never let me talk. It was always about her. And she has so many problems that I rather not share on a forum. Anyway, thanks for the advice.

XOXO,

Lorraine.

An almost instant message came back.

INCOMING MESSAGE FROM ANN1295:

Lorraine, just try again. Sometimes, mothers could use someone to be close with as well. It can't hurt to try to talk with your mother, right? You're welcome, baby girl. I just hope that you and your mother heal your relationship as well as healing your relationship with your best friend.

Yours Truly,

ANN1295

INCOMING MESSAGE FROM KITTY1242:

Maybe your best friend needs you just like you need her and you are letting her down. Have you ever been there for your best friend? Think about it for a second. I don't need an answer. I just want to know that you'll try to be there for her if you weren't ever there for her. Be there for her, Lorraine.

I would want my best friend to have done the same for me after we had a huge fight. Forgive and forget is how I look at your situation because if it really affects you, then you need to fix it yourself. Maybe your best friend is scared of losing you and just needs you to be there for her. So, be there for her. You'll regret it if you aren't there.

KITTY1242

I grab my keys, shut off my computer, and run down the stairs.

"I'll be right back, Mom." I leave before she can say another word about leaving without telling her where I am going. I drive to Katherine's house, hoping for a compromise. I'll accept being her friend if the gossiping stopped. *This* is the *only* compromise I am willing to make.

****

"Katherine!" I scream outside her house as I throw another pebble from the ground at her window. The front door opens and Katherine's older brother steps out.

"What the—Lorraine?" Brandon shivers before stepping outside and closing the door behind him. The rain had come close to a stop now and all that is left of its being is the sopping grass.

"What are you doing here?" He squints.

"I came to see Katherine. We left things pretty—" I stop throwing the rocks.

"I know. You should've seen her when she came home. I've never seen Katherine cry so much." He makes me feel guilty, his eyebrows furrowing with rage and understanding.

"Wow. I'm sorry."

"Don't say sorry to me. Say sorry to her." He brings his finger up to point to her window.

"I don't know—Lucas broke up with me." I stop myself before I say 'I don't know why I did it'. Because I do know why I did it; broken hearts break you. You get it from falling so hard. You choose if it heals or not. You make it heal or not. I was trying to get mine to heal but I'll always have that scar and I just have to accept that.

Heartbreak hurts but maybe it changes people for the better. It could teach you lessons on top of lessons. I learned that helping someone out is worth it, even if your job is on the line. I also learned by reading and replying to KITTY1242 and *ANN1295*'s messages that I should be closer with the people who surround me. I shouldn't push everybody away like I am starting to.

"Oh, Lorraine." Brandon opens his arms. I have always been small compared to the girls in our school who were '5'8'. Being only '5'5', it was nice to be engulfed into Brandon's arms because he is so much taller. I love being in someone's arms whether it be Lucas's or Brandon's and the new edition being Cooper's. But I don't love anything anymore because my heart is like a scrape. It's not healing right now. But I knew it would heal eventually.

"It's okay, really. I just shouldn't have taken it out on Katherine." I tell Brandon as I let his arms cave around me which has always been quite comforting.

"I get that but you didn't deserve that. Lucas has always been an ass but you really didn't deserve that. I hate that I was right." He brushes the hair out of my face.

"Well, you did say you would give me the benefit of the doubt when I first told you I was going out with him." I try to smirk through whatever pain is hurting me in my heart. I really could use someone to talk to right now.

"Yeah but it doesn't mean I wanted to be right. I wish I could've been wrong but I know Lucas. And I knew that he was going to run. He always does." He looks down at me.

"But something changed in him. I think he genuinely cared about me." I did not want to be called another one of his girls.

"Even though I hate to admit it, I think he did too." He sighs, clearly uncomfortable with the topic.

"Just go pull your sister out of bed." I shove him towards the house.

"Fine, fine. I'm going." He groans, entering his house and shutting the door, leaving me outside with the sky, illuminated only by the golden-yellow lamps hanging high above the ground.

As I stare at the racing car that passed by every so often, I grow anxious and fidgety as time drags on. I open my car door after I realize that Katherine is either standing me up on purpose or she is debating on whether coming out or not. Well, I hope me leaving makes her decision easier. Because once I leave, I am never coming back.

"Lor! Wait!" Katherine screams from behind me.

"What, Kat? I waited long enough. I'm not waiting anymore. And you know, I almost was going to say sorry to you." I stare at this red-eyed and tired-faced girl who I used to know.

"You know what's really funny, Kat? All I wanted was someone who could stand by me and be there for me. But you can't even do that, can you?" I chuckle, wickedly.

"I came here because I wanted my best friend back, but I don't think she's even *breathing* anymore." I growl before turning back towards my car and walking away from my friendship and my ex-best friend, Katherine Rose Xavier.

"Don't be like this, Lor. I didn't do anything." Katherine holds her hands up in surrender.

"That's exactly why I don't want you in my life anymore, Katherine. You didn't do anything." I throw myself into my automobile and put the key in the ignition. I am not going to let Katherine Rose Xavier bother me anymore.

So after I walk in my door once again, I collapse in my room and cry. But before I let myself cry, I edit the passage I had written and add pieces of what happened when I lost someone whom I could never get back now.

****

ENTRY:

When the first thing your best friend wants to know is the gossip of your relationship, you know something is up. But when all she wants to know is if it breaks off or not so she can tell the school, you know that something must be wrong with her. My best friend hasn't been my best friend since middle school, but she thought we were.

Today, she wanted to know the information about my break-up before making sure I was okay. While I was out of school for a week with a completely broken heart (my mother literally doesn't care what I do anymore), she didn't come to visit me once. I told her off and now I guess you could put her on my now-existent list of ex-best friends; a list that I've never had before in my life. And now that she's gone, I honestly don't know what I am going to do. But I know that I am better off without her. Because all she caused me was pain and she caused me to shiver whenever she was near. She broke me so deep that I didn't know anything else but that chaotic breaking.

But a stranger showed me today that there are people in the world who aren't looking to intentionally hurt you. I decided I needed a break from school and all of the misfortunes that had happened there that day. So I took a break at a diner by my house. But before that, you should know about the misfortune that happened today at school. Lucas, the one that had stepped on my heart spiraling it into a million tiny pieces, decided that he could do better than me and has a new girlfriend already. She is completely disrespectful for going out with my boyfriend right after we broke up but she is better looking than anything I've ever seen in my mirror. And he had the nerve to stare at me as he was passing by while I had the nerve to do the same. He isn't mine anymore; why am I still staring at this guy who broke up with me?

I stomped out of that school quickly but he followed me, gaining on my heels. He wanted to drive me to my house because I wasn't seeing clearly. But I told him to screw off and get the hell away from me. I drove home with red-eyes and a hurting heart, even though I knew I wasn't going to heal in a day. When I get home, the first thing that leaves my mother's mouth is, "Honey, what are you doing home?" I would think a mother should know that by instinct, when your daughter comes home crying, you don't ask her about what happened. I would hope that when I become a mother, if my daughter, God forbid, does go through what I am going through, that I wouldn't say what my mother did this afternoon. Not only did she say that but she also said that I loved my ex-boyfriend.

Love is a big word for me to comprehend. When I was little, I thought I would never love someone as much as I loved my mother and father. But clocks tick, times change and love becomes a great emotion that is used again, but not for family. It's used for people you practically don't know. My problem is that I fall in love too easily. With all my barriers up, I still manage to find my heart broken and still in love with the boy who left me without a word as to why. That's not what upsets me though. What upsets me is that he acts like we are still together. He comes to my house to check on me while I'm at the diner. You can't just do that. We are done, so let me heal and leave me alone.

The stranger I met while at the diner helped me heal the slightest bit so I can get by now. I know I will heal more throughout the weeks, but I can't help but think this stranger came over to me while working diner and risked his job just to make sure I was okay. Pure kindness doesn't come around every day as it should. This man showed me pure kindness and that I deserved better than a low-ranking-ass-of-a-guy as a boyfriend. He also showed me that there is more to life than finding someone to spend it with. There is adventure and lessons and dreams other than love coming true. I just have to dream big because not every book is a romance novel. This man that I met might not be able to follow his dream if he cannot get a scholarship to pursue it. He taught me that problems like that are the real ones, not a silly heartbreak that can easily be fixed. He is a man that has changed my life and will forever change it. I am going to try to visit him every day and write there from now on, because he has sparked a start in my writing. And he gives me inspiration to find what I really want to do with my life besides make it a romance novel. That is a book I am going to close for right now so I can focus on what matters the most: me.

XOXO,

Lorraine.

****

CHAPTER 2:

SECOND DAY GOING BACK TO SCHOOL SINCE THE HEARTBREAK:

Again: walking down the halls for the second time, feeling everyone's eyes on me. I can tell you it's not the best experience. I actually hate the attention. I hate it with a burning passion that is covered by a wish to be done with this school already. I am now seventeen. I hate my birthday. It is only my junior year but we are going into senior year soon. When we move on to senior year, I won't be the one that everyone will be staring at anymore. It won't be me. It will be a new girl or someone that has a good sob story people can latch onto and ridicule. Lucas Kelly will be out of this school for good and I will be free of his hold on me that he shouldn't even have.

I remind myself that it isn't about him anymore. It is me, myself, and I from now on and Lucas doesn't care about me, so I don't care about him.

"Lor!" I hear someone shout down the halls. My feet automatically quicken their normal pace because they know that Katherine will eventually catch up to me because of how fast she is. Katherine has always been the one to do better at sports. Her body was shaped better for it, stronger than I ever was. Doesn't mean I didn't try, but she would always get the medals and I would get the participation ribbons.

"Lor!" She shouts again and I start to run down the halls, trying to avoid her in whatever way I can.

"Stop running." She barely huffs as she grabs my forearm and pulls me into a classroom. Little did she know that there was a class going on.

"Sorry," she mutters to the class as I run out as quickly as I can. The bell suddenly rang, signaling that we both need to get to first period.

"I could miss first period just to talk to you, Lor."

Katherine gives me a grin as she catches up with me.

"Well, good for you. But I need to get to class. So leave me alone." I breathlessly say before walking down to my classroom and slamming the door behind me. It wasn't the right classroom but anything to get away from Katherine and her big ass speech that had been about to come.

****

BUZZ was the sound my phone made as I sat in an empty classroom for the period. I pulled my phone out of my pocket and it read:

INCOMING MESSAGE FROM KELLY2651:

Hiya, Lorraine. My name is Kelly, if you wanted to know. I read your blog, by the way. I mean, obviously. I think that it's really cool that you are writing and I think that it'll help you get your feelings out, sorta. It helps other people to know what kind of struggles someone else is going through for some odd reason. Guys don't understand what they do sometimes so I wouldn't blame your ex-boyfriend too much. It's our nature as guys to screw everything up; we need to add flaws to the women's flawlessness.

I understand he hurt your feelings but he's probably sorry and wants to mend things as much as you want to forget about things. I bet you are a really great girl and he messed up badly. Mend things with him is my advice. Even if you only become friends, afterwards.

XX&OO,

KELLY

REPLY:

Hi, Kelly. I'm sort of in withdrawal with my ex-boyfriend. I still like him but I don't know if that's enough for me to run back to him. After all, he broke my heart. Thanks for the advice though.

XOXO,

Lorraine

INCOMING MESSAGE FROM KELLY2651,

I'd really like to meet you one day. You are truly a strong inspiration and role model.
XX&OO,
KELLY

I sit there for a couple more minutes, thinking about what Kelly said to me. Though he made me feel really good about myself, I wasn't feeling good after my confrontation with Katherine and her quick feet.

I check through the window in the door of the classroom to see if Katherine stayed or not. When there is no sign of Katherine, I exit moving quickly and quietly. My feet automatically moved towards the school doors because I want to run away again; I want to run away every time I came into this school. But this time, I won't run away from Katherine or Lucas or myself. *I would stay here and fight*, I tell myself. I tell my legs to walk to U.S. History. And just like that, I am stronger already.

****

Finally, I stand up out of the last seat of the day. I almost sprint to my locker out of happiness. Trying not to shove people out of the way, I make it to my locker fairly quickly. A smile finds its way onto my face, brightening my day a little more to see a card hanging from my locker. I peel it off with ease and scan my eyes along each word:

Lorraine,

I wanted to tell you I am sorry. You know you are the only girl I've ever truly cared for. My feelings will always remain with you. I would tell you—I would tell you everything that was ever a secret about me. I love you with all my heart, Lorraine Hope Lowry. And I hope that one day when we are far from high school, we can be together. Just you wait and see, we will end up together.

"Did my heart ever love anyone before this moment? My eyes were liars, then, because I never saw true beauty before tonight."

Yours Truly…

There was only one person I know that quotes Shakespeare's, *"Romeo and Juliet"*. Then, there was a name scribbled out by the quote, but I already knew who it was from.

Lucas James Kelly.

****

I immediately collapse on the couch as my mother moves closer to inspect my appearance.

"How you feeling, kiddo?" Her hands are in death locks on her hips, a towel slung on her right shoulder. I knew that this was just an act but I decide to play along.

"Better than usual." I break out into a smile.

"I was just going to make some cookies; you want some?" My mother offers me as we move the conversation into the kitchen.

"Sure, I'd love some. I think I am going to go out for a while though." Cooper enters my mind. Around this time yesterday, a young stranger, quite like myself, walked up to me and offered me more help than he will ever understand; I wanted to see him again.

"Where to?" My mother inquires as I climb the stairs.

"I'm going down to Billy's with a friend of mine." I tell my mother before sliding my computer in my bag and throwing the charger in there, in case my Mac Book Air died. As I climb down the stairs with my bag in hand, I plague my mother: "Mom, could I get a job?"

I never thought about getting a job because my family has so much money already.

"Sure, sweetheart. If it's what you want. Happy Birthday." She turns towards me with a smile after putting the cookies in the oven.

"It's what I want. Thanks." For the first time in a long time, I actually had a normal and civilized conversation with my mother. Today is a day that makes you question, "What horrible thing is going to be sprung onto you?"

****

I left with cookies stuffed in my mouth and strength, which was an aura around me. As I drive off to Billy's, I think about seeing Cooper again. I think about the way he talked and the way he sat down and risked his job for me to take care of my wounds. Then, I think about the card I had received from my secret admirer, who I didn't think would go all the way out of his path to do something like that for me.

When I walk into Billy's Bar, the first thing I see is an empty bar. When I spot someone tending to the tables,

I notice the brown, combed hair and the muscular but skinny outline is all too familiar.

"I was wondering whether or not I could get a table in this place," I hide my voice with an accent as Cooper turns around and says, "Miss, you can—Lorraine?"

"Hi, Coop." I walk over towards him, giggling.

"I didn't except to see you here and so happy." Cooper smirks on his face at the sight of my happiness.

"Well, I've had a pretty good day."

"Nobody's here. I guess I could sit down for a while and I want to hear about that day you had. Then again, I could also just read your blog. Sit at your table and I'll bring you your coffee." He smirks, gesturing towards the corner booth where I had sat yesterday. I guess now it was my regular place to sit when I came to Billy's Bar; I like having a regular place where I belong.

"How do you know my coffee order?" Cooper puts his rag down and starts to make my latte.

"I know from yesterday. Did you not order a latte yesterday?" He asks me a rhetorical question.

"Sorry."

"It's okay. Two sugars, right?" He glances my way. I place my money on the table with ease.

"Yep." I pop the 'p.' My gaze fell on Cooper and for some reason, I couldn't pull my eyes off.

"You going to get to writing or are you going to stare at me all day?" He turns his head a bit to stare at my face.

"Sorry," I mutter, my face flustered from Cooper acknowledging my staring.

"It's okay. I just hope that you talk about your feelings for me in that blog of yours," He teases and tosses his rag around.

"Funny," I smirk at him.

"But I would be lying if I wrote that because I don't have feelings for you."

"You just hate to admit that you have a crush on the CAR." He makes the weakest muscle I've ever seen.

"You call that a muscle? I call that fat." He throws his rag at me as I catch it in the air. After shuffling my playlist, I move over to the bar to hand the rag back.

"Please Don't Go," by Joel Adams comes bursting through my computer as Cooper looks into my eyes.

"Nobody's here. You want to dance?" Cooper places his rag down.

"Right now?" A smile is glittering against my face.

"Sure, why not?" He glances at the door.

"Alright, sure." I take his hand that is reaching out for me.

"You know, I can't help feeling like I know you. Even though that has got to be the most cliché line in the world." He wraps an arm around my waist, his hand clutching my body against his, with a little space in between us because of the tension that we share. His chuckle makes me laugh with pleasure as he spins me around.

"Well, why do you connect with me the most?" I ask curiously, having to crane my neck up to look at his face.

"My girlfriend of two years was screwing my best friend and I walked in on it. So in some ways, I feel like I connect with you." He looks away from me to stare at the door, probably wishing he could leave and throw this conversation out the door with him.

"I'm really sorry, CAR."

"It's really okay. But the funny thing is that the day I met you was the day I walked in on them in a stall in the locker room." He laughs lightly, trying to break the tension because of the topic floating around in the room.

"It's not okay. But I guess that I healed you a bit too, right?" I hope, smiling again for increase in happiness of conversation.

"We are healing each other." He puts my hand that was once clutched in his, over his shoulder to attach to my other hand that was already resting there. His free hand went loosely around my waist as we swung back and forth in time with the music.

It is one of those moments you could almost refer to as perfect, though nothing in this world is actually perfect. Still, in this moment, I think nothing could ruin the way I am healed when I am with Cooper. The way he heals me; the way I heal him. There is nothing like a friend who knows what you've been through and decides to help you soar forward instead of float in the past.

Keep moving forward is the motto of today because I moved forward even if my mind and my legs were aching to walk out those doors. I keep moving forward with my heart trailing behind and eventually, I will become stronger.

"Cooper, get back to work or you'll be dancing unemployed," grins a woman with a black hat and apron, identical to Cooper's on. She has blonde hair, unlike Cooper, and her facial expressions look like she can't even kill a bug.

"Yes, ma'am." He takes my hand and spins me around before dipping me. The song isn't over but I understand that he needs to get back to his job.

"What the heck?" I laugh as I'm stuck in the position he dipped me in.

"I thought it would be cool if I dipped you." He holds me.

"It is cool. But there is a difference between dipping and holding me here until my back breaks." I laugh as Cooper realizes with wide eyes that my back hurts and he hoists me up, letting go of me.

"It's okay, Coop. Don't look so frightened. I think you should be more frightened of that woman who just told you to get back to work." I say, rubbing my back with my right hand.

"I've never been scared of Linda. She's been trying to boss me around forever but I never actually listen to her." He shrugs.

"What do you mean? You could get fired." I say, laughing softly.

"No. She could never fire me." He pushes it off.

"You're fired!" She screams walking out of her office.

"Linda, you can't fire me. In fact you need me to help you run this place." He says, before grabbing his rag and cleaning the counter for the 100th time today.

"You know I was kidding right, Cooper?" She asks, putting her hands on her hips in a frustrated stance.

"No. I thought you were serious." He says, sarcastically looking at me before rolling his eyes.

"Honey, you know I would never fire you. You are the best employee I have here." She says, smiling at him while his back was to her. I guess she doesn't know what sarcasm is.

"I'm pretty much the only employee you have here. Plus, I'm pretty sure my father wanted you to say that?" Cooper says, never even glancing up to talk to her.

"He did not, honey. Okay? I love your father. And he loves me." She lets go of her hips. Her fingers were clutched in tight fists, turning white with anger or the need to kill something by the looks of her face. Though, she stays calm.

"Are you sure? I mean he has been with a lot of women. Maybe his feelings are *confused*." Cooper says, without even flinching at his cruel words.

"Cooper." I say with a disappointed tone.

All Linda did was walk away and put her forehead in her hand, rubbing at it with sadness and frustration.

"What the hell was that?" I ask him, sitting down at the bar.

"I can't stand her." He rubs his own forehead, throwing the rag across the room.

"Your dad remarried to a nice woman. She gave you a job and she probably pays good. What is the big deal with that?" I ask him, my brows furrowed with understanding and confusion.

"She's trying to replace my mother. Nobody can take that role away from my birth mother. Okay? And she pays okay. But it's not like he married a woman with a stable house and stuff. He married a woman who went to jail for fraud and while my dad is in major debt. So now with my dad's amazing job, he's trying to pay back his debt. That's why I am never going to go to college. I can't afford it because my dad's more concerned with Linda and his problems than with his own son and going to college." Cooper explains, rubbing at his forehead again, feeling what I call hopelessness.

"I think you need the blog more than me." I tell him, then getting serious by saying, "Listen, I'm going to go talk to Linda and I'm going to get a job here. Okay? And all the money I make can go to your college fund. But you need to repair your relationships with your family because family is everything, okay? I have a horrible relationship with my mother and father and I wish I could fix it but they are both spoiled brats. I honestly wished I lived with you. The only family I sort of have is my brother, who is the most important person in my life. And just like you, I need to mend my relationships with everyone. But unlike you, I am the most stubborn person you will ever meet. But I can fix it if you can."

He spends a while debating the topic in his head before saying, "Okay. But I am not saying any half-assed bullshit to Linda. Nor will I ever because I never even wanted him to marry her in the first place."

"Just, do your job." I say, before smiling a bit and walking towards the room where Linda came from but stopping my tracks to ask Cooper a question: "Why don't you be more open about this?"

"If I were to be open with my feelings all the time, then I would be crushed all the time because you can't trust anybody. Broken hearts however, trust everybody. That's why it's so easy to talk to you. We are both broken and we are just looking for someone to lean on." He says, shooing me off after he was finished talking. I walk over to the room Linda came out of.

"Linda?" I ask trying to find her in the empty rooms near the restrooms.

"Linda?" I call out again, climbing stairs that led to a terrace.

"Linda?" I say again, walking out onto the terrace. A woman was crying in the corner of the terrace, her feet dangling off the edge.

"Linda?" I ask, advancing closer towards the woman. As I realize it is her, I sit down beside her even though I honestly know nothing about her except that she is in debt and she got arrested for fraud.

"Oh, honey what are you doing out here? I didn't hear the door." She said wiping her face and looking away.

"Linda, I don't know anything about you but I know a little something about Cooper. He's had a rough time lately and he doesn't mean to take it out on you. He just...he feels you are replacing his real mother. And he doesn't want that at all. His girlfriend cheated on him a couple of days ago and he doesn't think he can afford to go to college." I say not bringing up anything about her debt or her fraud.

"Thank you, sweetheart. I don't honestly know how his father and I are going to pay for his college. I just...I have to work hard to make the money." She rubs her forehead.

"Listen, I didn't want to tell Cooper this but...if you need help, I can get money. But you have to let me know how much and when. Okay? Just...speak to him and let him know that he doesn't have to feel like you're replacing his mother. And that you'll be there for him." I stand up and help her up as well.

"Thank you, darling. I think I really needed to just talk to someone for a bit. Even though you did most of the talking." She smiles brightly. I laugh before following her back to the bar where Cooper is supposed to be. Only Cooper isn't there anymore. He is gone.

****

I leave after Cooper had left. When I get home, my mother is sitting down at the table her hands folded, waiting for me.

"Hey, Mom." I say, adjusting the strap of my heavy bag.

"I was waiting for you to get home." She says obliviously with another glass of something in her hand, standing up and going up the stairs.

"Mom, is everything okay?" I ask her, before she starts to climb the stairs. I never usually ask her this but she has this weird look in her eyes that seems familiar to me because I usually have the same look in my eyes too.

"Of course, honey. We can talk about it tomorrow." She says lightly smiling before she continues up the stairs.

"Mom, what did I miss?" I ask, moving closer to the stairs.

She notices I am not going to stop until I know what she wants to tell me so she climbs back down the stairs and walks into the dining room, sitting down in the seat she was just in a minute ago.

I sit down in the seat next to her with my hands interlocked, my eyebrows folded with worry and concern.

"I'm worried about your brother. Your father isn't around a lot and I don't think he gets that quality time with someone. Can you just make sure you spend some more time with your brother during the week and on the weekends? He's getting lonely." She says, brushing back the hair that was in her face. But I knew she was getting lonely too.

"Sure, Mom." I say, smiling a bit before taking the hair tie out of my hair and massaging my stressed-out scalp.

"Thank you, Lorraine. Just...thank you." She said, putting an arm around me. When I hug my mother, I can tell she feels weak and tired. I take a guess that it is just because she lacked a lot of sleep but I don't want to keep telling myself that. I don't ask. Instead, I walk up the stairs, smiling at my mother before I close the door and get ready for bed. Opening my computer and turning it on, I plug in my phone letting it to charge. On my computer, a message popped up from Cooper. I quickly opened it, wanting to know where he ran to and why. It read:

I know I shouldn't have left but you shouldn't have talked with her. I don't want things to get better. I want them to stay the same because in my eyes, change is bad. I can't move forward with my life and in some ways; I don't want to. You asked me why I am not so open all the time and shit and that question really got me thinking, why am I not open? And then I remembered what happened with my best friend and my girlfriend. I thought when it happened I would never heal from that but I slowly starting to. And I think that with time, everybody eventually heals but with several cracks and bruises in their hearts, metaphorically.

Sometimes with feelings, you get confused about whether or not you exactly trust the person. Never lose sight of who you trust and who you don't because one day, someone who you don't trust but have feelings for is going to stomp on your heart just like she did mine. Lorraine, you are the only person I feel like I can trust. And that's pretty bad because I've only known you for two days but I feel like I've known you for my whole life.

You seem so familiar that it just doesn't seem possible for you to be an actual person.

See, you are what I call dream girls. Never forget that you are a beautiful and an independent woman who can accomplish anything she wants. I believe you can do whatever you choose to do in this world, not whatever comes your way. You make your destiny; people around you don't make it for you. Make your own destiny and be happy with it, Lorraine. You deserve it. I'm sorry for leaving and getting extremely off topic but sometimes it's easier to write than speak, as you have taught me with your blog. Maybe I should co-write with you. Anyways, I hope you figure out what you want to do with your life because it seems like a pretty bright one and I want to be there for it.

Coop

P.S: Look in your mailbox.

I quickly and quietly creep down the stairs and peek out the door. No one is there or down the streets.

The street just seemed eerie and empty whilst the yellow-lamp light that was illuminating the streets flickered consistently. Walking over to the mailbox, I immediately found a huge piece of paper that was laminated. How he knew where I lived, I'll never know.

You told me to draw you. So I drew you from my point of view.
XOXO,
Cooper.

I laugh at his reference to my endings of my blog entries. Bringing the paper inside, I actually start to take a good look at it when I lock the door. He drew me; you could clearly tell it was me, sitting at my corner booth, typing away on my computer while the latte that I ordered was sitting down beside me. I looked peaceful and calm with a smile on my face. I quietly walk up the stairs and closed my door like before. Clearing off everything else on my bulletin board and throwing it out, I pin Cooper's drawing in the middle of my bulletin. Smiling, I took a picture.

REPLY:

Yep, you are definitely going to art school. Where do you want to go? Did you look at how much tuition is yet?

INCOMING MESSAGE FROM COOPER:

I've been looking at Fashion Institute or maybe like New York University. But Queens College is probably a good choice because it has financial help which I need a lot. I haven't tried to look at tuition because I'm scared of the big numbers and I don't even have a financial plan yet. But I think if I had to pick one school to go to, it would be FIT because it is a really good school for the arts and stuff. Anyways, I have to see which ones I get into anyways. Maybe I'll get a scholarship or something.

REPLY:

I think it's perfect if you want it. We'll figure out money when it comes to the time to pay for it. I promise that I'll help you.

INCOMING MESSAGE FROM COOPER:

Thanks.

REPLY:

What do you want to be, Coop?

INCOMING MESSAGE FROM COOPER:

Something important. I haven't figured it out yet but I want to help people emotionally or something. I just don't know if art is the way to go for that.

REPLY:

You could teach art or create art. Try creating art, Coop. I think you would be really good at putting emotions into drawings. Maybe someone may actually like them as much as I do and buy them.

INCOMING MESSAGE FROM COOPER:

Yeah. You're funny.

REPLY:

I'm serious, Cooper. I would totally buy whatever you drew. Just take a shot at it and show me the progress you make. Okay? I have to get to bed. But I'll talk to you sometimes this week or maybe even stop by the Bar for a bit to do some writing.

INCOMING MESSAGE FROM COOPER:

Okay. Figure out what you want to do with your life, Lorraine. Your life is too special to not know what you want to pursue. College is in a year for you. Not that far but you should at least start thinking. Maybe even come with me to look when I go in like May. I want to get another feel before I make a decision. Plus, I have to work on my portfolio and the car ride there would be perfect to do that stuff. Plus, it's a road trip. Nobody says no to road trips.

REPLY:

Stop sucking me in, Cooper. It's bad enough I want to come.

INCOMING MESSAGE FROM COOPER:

Go to bed. We'll talk during the week. Goodnight.

REPLY:

Alright. Goodnight.

I shut my phone off and go back to my computer. Deciding not to post what I had wrote for today, I leave the message to move into tomorrow's space so that I can sleep. The clock says twelve a.m. and I am so tired that when I shut the lamp by my bed, I can't remember if I had changed out of my clothes from the day.

****

THIRD DAY GOING BACK TO SCHOOL SINCE THE HEARTBREAK:

I can't even wake up this morning. That's how tired I am. I roll out of my bed as my mother screams at me and throws me off my own mattress.

"Fine." I manage, rising off my stomach that is against my heated tile. I throw my hair up and put on different clothes. Deciding on a t-shirt and jeans with black boots, I slip on a sweatshirt and leave before my mother could yell at me anymore, grabbing an apple on my way out.

Jumping in my car, I drive slowly with eyes wide open to school. When I park and shut off my car, I sit there listening to music off my phone and eating the apple I had snatched. I put my head against the steering wheel and take a couple of minutes for myself before getting out of the car and walking into Bay Ville High, Home of the Bears.

****

"Lorraine!" A person calls out as I am walking down the halls. I'd like to not be bothered but today, I am getting bothered by the worst person possible.

"Hey, I went by your house the other day to make sure you were okay but you weren't there." He puts his hand up against my locker to make sure I was listening and to catch his breath.

"Okay. Can I help you?" I ask, not looking at him.

"Look at—" His famous line was relaying in my head over and over again.

"NO." I say pretty loudly without realizing it and turn to walk down the hall opposite way, slamming the locker as I left.

"Lorraine, why?" He asks, holding my forearm.

I shook him off and said, "You should be asking yourself that question. You broke up with me." I snicker and walk away with guilt for making the boy who broke my heart feel like crap. I should be the one feeling like crap because I still continue to put the pieces back in his hands, hoping that he will fix me. But he won't because he's not mine anymore. And he doesn't realize but he never will be again. I can guarantee that. At least, I think I can.

"Lorraine, come on. Just talk to me like a person." He says grabbing my forearm again.

"What the hell would you even want to talk about, Lucas? There is nothing to say. It's over. You said it pretty clear when you broke up with me. I don't need for there to be a second time, especially if it's in public." I say shaking my arm out of his grip and walking back down the halls. Lucas pulls me into the classroom on his right without my consent.

"What the hell—" I yell before Lucas covers my mouth and pulls me back against him, covering the door.

"Get the hell off of me!" I scream, getting out of his grip.

"You can't do this and then expect me to not care, Lucas. You broke up with me. This is freaking nuts." I put my head in my hands and sit down in one of the desks.

"Listen, Lorraine. I'm trying to make it better between us. I really am. I didn't want to break up with you." He says kneeling down beside the desk I am sitting at.

"Are you high?" I ask him the legitimate question.

"No. I'm serious. Lorraine, I love you so much." He says for the first time ever, grabbing my hand on one knee.

"Lucas, you can't do this to me." I say holding my head, my eyesight getting foggy from tears once again like the first day.

"Lorraine, we can fix this. Just help me get rid of April." He continues to hold my hand.

"Stop embarrassing yourself, Lucas." I say turning away and biting my lip to avoid a sudden breakdown.

"I know you love me too. You have to. I still see the way you look at me, Lorraine. Tell me you don't feel that." He puts my hand against his chest, to touch his heart.

"Stop." I whisper, suddenly breaking down.

"Oh, Lorraine. I'm going to make it better." He holds my head and brings it closer to his chest.

"Cooper..." I whisper wrapping my arms around Cooper. I look up and see Lucas instead. I push Lucas back and hold my hand against my mouth, in shock. I need Cooper.

Sometimes when you go through something really bad, as heartbreak, you latch onto someone for guidance and reassurance so that you can move forward. And in that moment, that person is the best thing in your life. Cooper is the best thing in my life right now.

"Cooper? Who's Cooper?" Lucas steps back after I push him away from me.

"Someone who would never make the same mistakes you keep on making." I get up out of my seat.

"Listen, Lorraine. I love you." Lucas says, advancing towards me. My instincts kick in and all of a sudden, my hand shoots out, smacking Luke across the face.

"I-I'm so sorry." I say sobbing into my hand before drawing in a deep breath. "You just don't get to say that."

"But it's true." He says moving closer to me. I want to run out of this room but I know I have to stay and finish this conversation or I would forever regret it.

"Luke, this isn't the Notebook because I clearly don't like you back anymore." I say pulling his hands off of mine. Putting my leg over my left leg and placing my elbow on my thigh to support my head on my hand, I laugh inside at how weird this situation is.

Luke doesn't say a word. He just quickly exits the room, leaving me with nothing but my crowded thoughts and my mind that is filled with chaos, just like my world.

****

I walk into the bar, needing Cooper's automatic healing now more than ever.

"Cooper!" I scream recklessly into an empty bar. It was one o' clock in the afternoon and I skipped school just so I could see Cooper, though I didn't know if he would be here or not because he had a school as well.

"Linda?" I call out curiously. Heels pounded loudly against the floor as they moved closer and the woman making those sounds came out of a room.

"Hey, babe. What's up?" She asks stuffing her hands in the back pockets of her jeans.

"Listen, where is Cooper?" I advance towards her with two steps.

"He's still at school. Why?" She asks curiously, turning her head.

"Nothing...Thanks!" I say running out of the bar quickly. I drove to Lakewood High with only the need for Cooper and his beautiful words, not realizing I was entering dangerous ground.

****

I sit in my car for a minute and shot a quick text message to Cooper.

Can you spare a few minutes? Come outside the school.

INCOMING MESSAGE FROM COOPER:

I'll be there in a second.

I get outside of my car and lean against it, waiting for Cooper.

"Hey, babe." Someone says from behind me. I turn around and a group of guys are standing across from my car, smoking whatever drug they are high on right now.

"If you are looking for something, you can't get anything from of me." I move over a bit as they advance towards me.

"But I think I can." One says grabbing my arm.

"Let go of me." I say trying to get my arm out of his tight grasp.

"I don't think so." One of them said grabbing my other arm.

"Let go of me before I scream rape." I pull my arms towards me.

"Honey, you can't scream rape if you aren't getting raped." Another one says grabbing my hips and moving towards my face.

"Get off of me." I scream, busting my arm out of one of their grasps and hitting the one in the middle across the face. He holds his face and smirks.

"You really shouldn't have done that." He says punching me in the stomach before kissing my face.

I bend over in pain as he pulls my face up to his. I moan in pain against his bone-dry lips. When he stops kissing me, he smacks me across the face, leaving a permanent sting.

One of the boys that was holding my arm disappeared in a split second. I turn my head, looking at Cooper who is standing off to the side, throwing one of them on the ground.

"Coop." I call out grateful. I gain my arm back just to punch the one kissing me in the face.

He is thrown back in pain and the one holding onto my arm let go instantly.

"You can throw a good punch, baby." The one that kissed me says, his mouth bleeding as he winces, touching it with his forefinger.

"Don't call her baby. She's not yours, Marcus. And she never will be. Do you know how long I have been waiting to do that?" Cooper growls, punching Marcus in the face just like I had done.

"Cooper, come on." I call him over before he could do collateral damage to Marcus. Cooper's hand made a tight fist before he unclenches it.

"You're not worth it." He spits in his face and gets off of him. He advances towards me and wraps his arms around me.

"Are you okay?" Cooper kisses my forehead.

"I'm fine." I lie, holding my stomach in pain.

"Come on. Let's get the hell out of here." He moves into the driver's seat, not letting me drive.

I smirk, even though the sting from the smack made me want to keep a straight face. I move into the passenger seat and put my head against the seat as Cooper drives away.

I am weak once again and I hate it.

****

CHAPTER 3:

"Are you sure you are okay?" Cooper asks helping me into the bar.

"I'm fine. I just have to go to the bathroom." I wait for him to give me directions to the bathroom in the bar.

"First door on the left." He points towards the hallway.

He lets me go and I walk on my own, fighting the pain and the anger inside me. I shut the door, letting out a sigh that was shaky as soon as the door clicked. I slide against the wall next to the door, my butt hitting the cold tile floor that was probably filthy. I lift my shirt up and a little fist sized black and blue was forming where I was hit in the gut. I laugh shaking in the process, my giggles turning into sobs. While standing up almost falling over, I take a good look in the mirror and see a huge red welt forming on my face from the smack. I watch in disbelief as it swells. I smile in pain, laughing when the pain became too much. Tears burned the irritation that was forming.

I splash water on my face hoping that I could stop sweating from nerves. I tie my hair back in a bun and stare in the mirror for a while, wondering how I let myself be weak once again. When I created a bang sound against the door while I was trying to sit down, Cooper became worried.

"Lorraine, you okay?" He turns the door handle a bit.

"You can come in." I say, sitting back down next to the door so it would be able to open.

"Hey, are you okay?" Cooper asks, closing the door behind him and sitting down next to me.

I look at his face before saying, "Not really." Tears formed in my eyes and I knew I shouldn't let them fly but I couldn't hold them back as much as I tried. Sometimes, when I try to hold back crying so hard, a knot forms in my throat and most times, I can put up with it. But this wasn't one of those times.

"Oh Lorraine, I'm--"

"Just don't." I say, taking in a shaky breath.

"I'm so sorry." He says leaning my head against his shoulder.

"It's okay. I just-I'm just tired of feeling weak." I say smiling a bit at the wall.

"What are you smiling at?" He asks, curiously.

"How the hell does this always happen to me? Bad things, I mean?" I ask him as if he actually knows the answer. "Sometimes, bad things have to happen to good people in order for the good things to seem good." He says, trying to explain something that is unexplainable. But he did a good job of explaining something that not even the great philosophers could.

"It sucks but sometimes, in order to have a good outcome in the end, you have to have a bumpy road." He furrows his eyebrows.

"You are so cheesy." I laugh a bit.

"I know but you love me." He smiles.

"I don't know. I've only known you for a couple of days, Coop." I look shocked and then laugh it off.

"That's true. But we have learned to know each other in this short amount of time and I can't believe I'm saying this to a stranger, but I think you are my best friend." He leans his head against the top of mine.

"Well I think you are my best friend and sadly, I tend to love a little too easily. So yes, I probably do love you."

"You know that Lucas talked to me today? That's why I came to find you." I say my smile dropping at the thought of Lucas.

"Oh, yeah? What did he want?" He takes his head off of mine to look at me. I look at Cooper.

"What did he say?" Cooper asks me after I wait to piece together what Luke even wanted in the first place.

"He told me he loves me." I say shrugging and bringing my knees up, hugging them.

"He told you he loves you?" Cooper asks his voice louder standing up quickly to stare at my face.

"Yeah he did. Why?" I could feel my face getting red from a blush that was creeping up it.

"Lucas Kelly doesn't tell people he loves them without actually caring for them. Okay? I've never heard of any girl who was told by Lucas Kelly that he was in love with them." Cooper says pacing, pointing fingers and thinking.

"What's the big deal, Coop? He said he loves me not that he's *in love* with me." I said itching the other side of my face, the one without the welt.

"And what's the difference?" He sits across from me.

"When you say I love you, you can be really good friends and have a relationship that is *just friends* but when you say I'm falling in love with you, you genuinely want to be with that person romantically and sometimes, you can experience it and it's the best thing in the world but it can also break your fucking heart." I explain as Cooper listens carefully as quiet as a mouse for some reason. I just randomly start picking the dirt out from under my nails.

"Wow...you know a lot about love, don't you?" He smirks.

"I've only been in love once and sadly that was with Lucas." I frown.

"I think you guys are amazing together so I'm rooting for you and Luke but as your friend, I have to say shit like: 'For a girl as amazing as you, you'll have another shot at it with a really amazing guy. I know it.' But if I was that guy, oh damn."

I laugh loudly feeling the pain of the welt and the bruise that is forming on my stomach.

"Don't laugh. It's not funny. I would treat you as if you are freaking Miss America." He says bowing down to me.

"You're so weird." I try to stand.

"Hold on, let me help you." He says getting up and reaching out for my hands to help me up.

"Thanks." I say taking his hands as he pulls me up. I fell face first into his chest.

"Are you okay?" He grabs my face in his big hands.

"Ouch." I wince from the welt.

"Oh, jeez. We should put something on that." He says grabbing my waist and pulling me into the bar part of Billy's. A few customers had walked in but Linda was behind the bar serving for them.

"Linda, you didn't have to. You could have called me out." Cooper goes behind the bar to help her. I sit down at the bar this time instead of at my corner booth so that I could put a warm towel against my face and talk to Cooper.

"It's okay. I didn't want to disturb you and I think that the pretty girl over here could use you more than I could." She winks at me as Cooper ties his apron on and throws his hat on.

I smile then, I stop because of the welt on my face that was starting to swell.

"What happened to your face?" Linda watches my face with concern.

"I got punched." I sigh.

"Oh my goodness. Are you okay?" She gets me a clean towel drenched in warm water while Cooper looks at Linda from the corner of the bar and smiles. This is the first time I've seen him smile around Linda.

"What's your name, darling?" Linda asks me as she waits for my name.

"Lorraine." I smile as I take the cloth from her and hold it against my face.

"Lorraine...pretty name for a pretty girl." She winks at me before putting her elbows down on the bar, waiting for a normal conversation with me.

"Thank you." I smile at Linda for her kindness towards me even though she didn't even know my name.

"You got it, darling. I'm just glad you're there for Coop." She winks at me and continues to stand by me.

"I'm glad I'm there, too. But I'm just repaying a debt; he was there for me even when I thought it wasn't possible for a simple stranger to show such kindness to another."

"Honey, considering everything he's been through, I guess nice has come naturally. I mean I heard his mother was a wonderful person but between you and me, his father and I show no kindness that he would ever want to learn. I'm telling you there is no worse role models than his father and I." Linda gets back to scrubbing the counter with all of her arm strength.

"I'm sure he has learned some of it from you. When I first met you, I thought you were the nicest bosses I have ever met." I offer trying to make the situation any less awkward but knowing in fact that Cooper's father and Linda were the worst parents that any child could have.

Changing the subject before she could respond, I said, "Look, how hard would it be for me to get a job here? It doesn't have to pay at all but I'm trying to pay back what Coop did for me. I just have to—"

Linda extends her hand and replies, "You just got the job."

"I didn't even try out yet." I say, smirking a bit at her sudden outburst.

"I have seen you in here for a couple of days now and I'm pretty sure I'll see you in here for the rest of your days. So you might as well have a job here so Cooper isn't always nagging me to hire more employees." She laughs as I join in with her, the sound of our laugher making Cooper's head snap around to smile at us.

"You know I think if he didn't have a strong disliking for you because of the ring on your finger, he would actually accept you as the person you are. Because in all honesty Linda, he actually likes you. He is just scared to admit it and scared to stop pretending to hurt your feelings and crap." I balance my chin on my elbow, watching Cooper as he pours drinks and took orders, running back and forth.

"I can't solve that though. It's himself that he is struggling with. Not me. And if he wants to take it out on me, that's fine. Just as long as he lets it out somewhere. I don't want him doing bad things out in the middle of nowhere like I used to do." She says as a person sits next to me and gives Linda his order.

"Hey, Lorraine?" Linda calls out from behind the beer fountain. She was a short person so her face was almost hiding behind the fountain.

"Yeah?" I ask, getting off of the comfortable seat that had imprinted my butt cheeks in the cushion.

"Today's your first day. Show me whatcha got, girlie." She says before sliding the beer across the bar to the man next to me, like you see in the movies. The only problem with this moment is I knew nothing about alcohol.

****

"I got it!" I laugh at the fact that I am learning how to open a beer bottle. My attempt at the past couple of ones has been void but I have been making progress because of the way Cooper keeps nodding at me.

"Okay! Just open the bottle, Lorraine." He waits for the same moment I am waiting for; for the popping sound to signify that I actually opened the bottle. I shut my eyes tight as did Cooper whilst silence filled the air, waiting for a sound that was at the peak of springing.

As the pop of the top of the bottle sounds, I cheer loudly and yell as Cooper picks me up and turns me around in the air. Wouldn't you do the same if you spent a half-hour trying to teach someone how to open a beer? That is only a beer cap, imagine how long it's going to take me to learn how to actually make drinks.

"I think we should just keep you to beer bottles, fountain drinks, and food." He laughs.

"I know how to make a shot of tequila?" I offer, before busting into laughter with Cooper.

"That's the easiest thing to make in the industry of bartending." Cooper says before wiping down the counter and pulling two glasses out from under the bar. He pours half of the beer into each glass.

"How can you bartend if you are underage?" I ask wondering if someone would know I was underage.

"Nobody ever asks for my age. Plus I look like I'm in college. I don't think it actually matters. I'll be out of here sooner or later." He says before taking a swig of the beer that I had successfully opened all by myself.

"True. True." I say as Cooper slides the beer closer to me.

"Take a sip, it won't kill you." He picks the glass up for me and brings it to my lips before pouring the slightest bit down my dry throat. I cough before swallowing the bitter and horrible liquid as the contents work their way through my body.

"Tell me that was bad and that you never want to drink it again." He says, taking another swig of his glass that was now a quarter from being empty.

"That was awful. How do humans drink that stuff?" I ask Cooper before he replaces his now empty glass with my somewhat full one.

"Have you ever heard the expression of 'drowning one's sorrows?'" He asks me before looking at the beer with amazement.

"Coop, I think you had enough of that stuff tonight. It's time for you to close up and get home." I say, before pulling the glass of beer out of his hand and dumping the contents into the sink that was next to me. I know a person who is an alcoholic and I didn't want Cooper to turn into one at such a young age. He has so much potential in life.

"Lorraine!" He shouts, startling me out of the deep slumber I was falling into from the day that I spent taking orders and pouring fountain drinks for little kids.

"Why did you do that?" He asks, staring at the now empty glasses that joined the others in the sink from the long day of work.

"Because you already had one glass. You didn't need another. You need to close up anyways." I add, fixing my hair into a messy bun so I could help close up.

"I'm fine." Cooper says, walking towards the front door.

"And where do you think you are going?" I ask him, my hand sturdy on my hip. If only he knew I was trying to help him.

"For some fresh air." He says, before stepping out of the bar and into the cold night. As I watch him sigh, I watch the carton dioxide that looked like fog escape his body. His girlfriend had cheated on him and I had never asked about it, thanks to my problems. But I should have. Because while he was walking away, his body said it all.

"I'm hurt and you could've fixed me."

Guilt collides with the bile in my throat as I call the one number that is left on the fridge for emergencies.

"I need your help." I say into the phone. Because right when Cooper left, I heard footsteps in the other room. Someone is in the bar with me.

****

Immediately, I tell Linda on the other line that someone is in the bar. She said to get the hell out of there but my instincts told me to stay and save Linda's bar, the only thing she has left that makes her money. Without the bar, I don't think she would be able to survive. I took the cake-cutting knife from the utensil drawer. As I hold the knife in my hand, my heart beats faster than ever before and Linda goes ballistic on the other line. And just like that, I hit the end button on my phone. Quickly, I dial Cooper's number only to get voicemail. I shut the phone off.

I slip my phone in my pocket and hold the knife in a tight grip as the footsteps became louder and closer as I move towards them, trying not to make any noise myself. A thump echoes from down the hall, throwing me off track. I bump into a box, knocking over a whole box of papers that were in neat stacks. I curse under my breath and promised myself that if I ever made it out of here, that I would clean that up for Linda.

As I say a prayer under my breath, I approach the footsteps with a great amount of caution. The footsteps sounded occasionally now only making a light banging noise once in a while. As I take another step towards the door, the floorboard creaks from under me. In a split moment, I hid against the wall on the side of the door, just to make sure that if the footsteps did open the door to the room, I wouldn't be seen. Taking a deep and silent breath, I open the door and hide again against the wall, hoping that whoever is making the noise would come out and face me like a man.

With not even a sound from the room anymore, I take another deep breath and step in the door way, holding out the knife as my defense. But as I scanned the perimeter, nobody was there. Or so I thought.

****

Pounding. That's all I could hear. Frightened. That's all I could feel. Blackness. That's all I could see. Dryness. That's all I could taste. Ropes. That's all I felt against my skin. The rubbing of the rope against my skin was giving me rashes, but that was the least of my worries. When my eyes slowly opened, I noticed the environment around me. I was still in the bar but I was in a part that I have never seen before. The stock room. Boxes of alcohol were lined up against the walls, crowded into just about every space in the room besides the middle of the room; that was an open space. A guy was sitting on one of the whiskey boxes, checking out the cake-cutting knife that used to be in my hand for defense. Now, it was in some guy's hand for offense.

"Who are you?" I ask the man in the darkness, who looked up to take a peak at my face.

"Someone you don't want to mess with." A female voice came out, the body standing up and advancing closer into the moonlight that was coming in through the window. Just like a horror movie.

"Have you ever been afraid, Lorraine?" The woman/man asks me walking in a circle around me. My eyes followed the figure that still wasn't visible.

"Yes." I reply, staring at this figure who thought that he or she had control over me.

"Have you ever been so scared that you just wished that you could be able to take it all away with something as simple as a knife? Something like a drink or a simple blade that could cut your skin in an instant?" She says, digging the blade lightly into her finger. She winced and groaned a bit but pulled the knife tip out of her finger before it could go in any deeper.

"No." I say, watching her movements that were slow and timed. Blood is visible on her finger from her little poke.

"Have you ever felt pain, Lorraine? Or has it been just heartbreak and not getting everything you want? Life doesn't always go your way, Lorraine." She gets closer to me.

"How do you know my name?" I ask her realizing this person knew my name, my family, and Lucas.

"I know a lot about you, Lorraine. I've been watching you. What if I had taken Cooper instead? Imagine that." She says, laughing this horrid laugh that made me want to cry. But I didn't. After this girl asking me about weakness and being scared, I thought crying would just add to her chilling urge for murder.

"What do you want from me?" I ask, not showing any signs that I am at all scared of her or him.

"I want you to scream. I want you to call for help. And try to struggle out of those bands that I tied so tight, you probably can't breathe. I want you to be terrified." She says, stepping into the shadows.

"What are you scared of?" I ask, trying to find a weakness in the person that was trying to get me to be scared of her or him.

"I'm not scared of anything." The person says, taking a step back to sit down on the whiskey boxes. They were lying and it was clear, thanks to their sudden change in their voice.

"I can tell from your voice that you're lying. You're scared of something. That's why you are taking it out on me. Because you don't want to take it out on yourself. I bet if you—"

"You don't know anything!" She screams at me chucking the knife that I once held into the side of the whiskey box.

"I think I do. You're scared. You want to feel strength or power over someone so that you won't feel scared for at least a moment but in all honestly, if you kill me, it won't make you feel any better. In fact, if you have blood on your hands, it'll make you feel worse. Once you have the blood on your hands, it never comes off. It follows you around for the rest of your life. Even in your sleep. So if you want to kill me, kill me. But just know that murdering me will be in the back of your mind for the rest of your life and that scared feeling that is in the pit of your stomach right now, won't go away once I do. It'll get bigger. I can promise you that." I finish watching as she takes the knife and throws it on the floor.

"I never was aiming to kill you. I was just aiming to put you in the hospital. You need to get off the streets and out of people's lives. You are just a monster, aren't you?" She asks me, moving closer to my face.

If there was one thing I hated most of all, it was name-calling. I couldn't stand it and for some reason, this girl knew it. She knew how to get to me and my weaknesses. She knew it all and I didn't even know her.

Now, her whole body became visible in the moonlight. This girl, who is now verified as a girl, is wearing a white spaghetti strapped tank top and light blue washed jean shorts. Her white shoes are covered in dirt and her face was covered with a plastic clown mask.

I laugh at the fact that this person knew me well enough to know that I have coulrophobia, a fear of clowns.

"What? You don't like clowns?" She laughs again. Her body, laugh, and voice are all too familiar for my liking.

"I know you, don't I? And we used to be friends, didn't we? But what happened? Remind me." I tell the figure who knew that I know she looked familiar.

"I remember perfectly, Lorraine. The question is do you remember?" She pulls off the mask before taking the knife that is in the whiskey box and hitting me in the head with the handle of the knife. I black out instantly.

****

"KATHERINE!!!!!" I wake up palms and back sweating while screaming for someone I knew is definitely my ex-best friend. My head was pounding with such a burning sensation, I thought I was going to pass out again.

Katherine Rose Xavier is a stranger to me. In fact, she isn't even a stranger. She is a person, who I didn't want to know, didn't want to see. I lean back against the head of the bed I am laying on. What the hell is going on?

"Hello?" I call out looking for someone.

The room I am in is empty. I stand up on my own two feet with a bad headache. Was the nightmare that I went through just an illusion created by my mind? Or did it actually happen? I search the room for some sort of telephone or maybe a key because the door is completely locked.

"Hello?" I call out a little louder so that if anybody is outside the door, they could hear me. But still, nobody answers.

Scavenging the room for anything I could use to get out of this room, I sigh and throw a box against the wall in frustration. The box opens and inside is a small key.

I pick up the key and examine it. It is small but it looks big enough to open the door that is blocking me from the outside world. I turn the key in the door and hear a clicking sound. Quickly, I turn the doorknob and walk out into the bar.

What the hell was going on?

"Hello?" I scream this time, searching for anyone. Surely enough, Linda steps out of another room.

"Lorraine!" Linda screams and clutches me in her arms.

"What happened?" I ask Linda.

"You called me and said that there was someone in the bar. I rushed over as soon as I could but there is nobody here, Lorraine."

"Did you hear anything while I was on the phone with you? Anything in the background?" I ask her because I'm just as confused as she is right now.

"No, you shut off the call." She sits down on a chair that is next to the bar.

"I don't know if it was a dream or not but I saw my ex-best friend here. I don't know if it's true but I know something happened and I just can't remember what exactly." I sigh sitting down on the chair next to her.

"Well, we can check the security footage. I only have cameras outside, in the bar, and in the inventory room." She says, pointing down the hall to the inventory room.

"Well, I think I was in the inventory room so we can start there." I say, before we walk down to the inventory room to watch the footage.

****

After putting a starting point on the time, we just sit there and wait for something to happen. As time passes on, motion starts to be seen through the camera.

While watching, we see a person walk in with a body on his back. The person then places the body on the chair and ties her up as she sits there, unconscious with a bag over her head. As the person sits there with knife in hand, the girl in the chair never wakes up. Eventually, the person with the knife gets tired of waiting, and scratches her arm with the knife to see if she will wake up from pain before hitting the girl in the head several times with the back of the knife because she won't wake up. After he waits a little longer, the body still does not show life so he carries her out of the room and takes the bag off of her head.

The tape gets paused by Linda as she looks over at me. I pull up my sleeve and show her the scratch on my arm, identical to the one in the video. I am the victim in the chair and we now have footage of the person who attacked me. But it didn't look like Katherine at all.

"He wasn't aiming for you." Linda says, right away, defending the man who attacked me.

"How do you even know that?" I say with an attitude, looking over at her.

"Because that guy," She says, pointing to the man in the mask with the knife, "Used to be my husband."

"No fucking way, Linda. Why the hell would your ex-husband do that?" I stand up and exit the room, pushing my hair out of my face, frustrated.

"This is his way of revenge; I did something bad to him first." She says, following me out of the room where truth came together.

"None of this makes any sense!" I scream, rubbing at my tired eyes even though I have makeup on. I could feel the makeup streaming down my face as tears soon follow. I suck them up and put my forehead against the bar.

"I'm sorry, honey." Linda says, pushing the hair behind my head and then tying it with a hair tie.

"Please, just don't." I say, walking out of the bar and taking in a deep breath of the cold air. The wind blew by and so did time. I hadn't even realized what time it was. I pull my phone out of my back pocket and call my mother.

"Lorraine! I was so worried!" My mother says first thing when answering the phone. But I know she is just lying and covering up all her aggravated emotions.

"I know, Mom. I'm okay. I won't be back home for a while. I can't tell you why but we will talk when I get home. I'm sorry." I say, pulling the phone away from my ear and listening to the screams from far away that came through the phone.

I put the phone back to my ear and said, "I know, Mom. I'm sorry and I love you. Just go to bed. I'll be home soon, I promise." I shut the phone off and slip it back into my pocket.

I let the cold air take my thoughts and worries away. I hadn't seen Cooper since he walked out. *Maybe I could find him*, I thought before sleeping on the front steps of *Billy's Bar*.

****

It was freezing when I woke up. Linda beside me wrapped a blanket around me, a mug in her hand, filled to the top with hot coffee.

"I thought you could use some of this," She offers me a smile, though I was still pissed at her for what had happened in the inventory room.

"Thanks," I take the mug with a dry throat and drink the cup in increments.

"Look, I'm really sorry but I would like it if you didn't tell Cooper it was my ex that did this. It will just make him hate me even more and I don't need that right now, not while I'm trying to gain his trust and love."

"Cooper's not even talking to me right now so I wouldn't worry about that. He stormed out on me last night because I threw out the beer he was drinking." I huff, not wanting to tell her about anything more than the simple stuff. Things were getting complicated with Cooper and I just wish he would talk to me.

"He's been taking from my liquor collection for a couple of days now. He's been needing to 'drown his sorrows,' I think. I was meaning to talk to him about it but I'm sure he will come around and talk to you. Maybe he just needs some time." She puts her arm around me and smiles before leaving me there and walking inside *Billy's*.

"It's not that I don't want to talk. It's that I never really talk about myself a lot. It's always been everyone else before me and I like it that way." Cooper says, stepping out from around the alleyway next to the bar. He moves to sit down next to me, his hands crushed into his pockets.

"Why didn't you just tell me that instead of walking out?"

"I was half-drunk and slurring and worried that if I say how I truly feel I'll get so attached that it will make me want you even more than I already do. I mean you did save me and when someone saves you, you feel drawn to them." He explains, looking at the busy streets and listening to the chirping birds in the morning.

"I know exactly how you feel," I tell him, bringing my eyes to gaze upon him before explaining to him all about how I slept on the steps, leaving out everything from the attack to who did it.

****

Linda tells me to go home and talk to my mother, though I don't want to. I eventually go home and talk to my mother about where I was so that she doesn't worry about me getting caught up in the wrong stuff or the wrong people. After I make sure that her and my brother were set, I go back over to *Billy's Bar* to work the night shift. Not seeing Cooper or Linda in the bar, I sit outside the steps and wait for Cooper or Linda to arrive.

A bing came from my phone a few seconds later though.

INCOMING MESSAGE FROM COOPER:

I need your help.

REPLY:

Where the hell are you, Coop?

INCOMING MESSAGE FROM COOPER:

Behind the bar in the alleyway. Come quick.

I didn't even have time for a reply because I ran so fast to the back of the bar, throwing my phone into my back pocket once again. I stop when I see a body against the dumpster, phone beside him.

"Cooper?" I ask, walking towards him.

"No, run Lorraine." He manages, spitting up blood in the process.

"Why would I leave you? We have to get you up and out of here. I'm sorry for not having texted you, dammit. I should have texted you." I say, kneeling down next to him.

"What happened to you?" I ask Cooper as he takes my arm and throws his body on top of me.

"Cooper, what the hell are you–?" And then I saw him. The guy that came after me on the footage. His familiar terrifying clown mask. He came after Cooper too. I scream the loudest I could for help as the man dug a dagger through Cooper.

"Cooper!" I shriek loudly. His eyes go wide as the pain gets in and he begins to stare at the floor beside my head. He spits up blood all over me but I didn't care.

"Why are you doing this to us?" I tell the guy who took the knife out of Cooper.

"Because Linda did the same thing to me." He says, sounding so familiar, before he walks away and drops the knife on the floor. As soon as he is nowhere near the alley way, I pull out my phone and call 911. I roll over so that Cooper is with his back on the floor.

"Cooper, you are going to have to keep looking at me. You have to stay awake." I tell the 911 operator all the information she needs.

"Cooper, look at me." I say, holding his face and moving it to look at me. His eyes are no longer wide, his beautiful smile still on his face.

"Keep looking at me. Stay awake, Cooper. Don't leave me." I say tears flooding down my face. He looks up at me and occasionally blinks while I tell him sweet words and recall the good memories we had in just four days.

"Cooper, stay awake." I say putting my hand on his face and turning his face toward me.

"It's okay. I'm happy." He says, his eyelids sinking, but a smile still on his face.

"Cooper, don't leave me here. Please." My lip quivering.

"It should've been me. I hurt everybody I touch." I mutter before putting my head on Cooper's chest.

"No, it felt good to save you. Although, it did hurt for a couple of minutes. You didn't hurt me when you touched me, you made me feel more alive than I have ever felt in my life. Now, all I see is your beautiful face. And I'm okay leaving with that image in my head." He says smiling a bit at me even though there was a huge hole in his side. He strokes the side of my face as tears wipe my makeup off my eyes.

"But you always saved me. I never got a chance to save you and I'm so sorry that I never did." I say crying into his undershirt that was red with blood. His arm crawled up my spine and hugged me closer to him. I could feel the blood on my face but I didn't care. I didn't feel it right now. Right now, I felt numb.

"It's okay. You saved me even though you weren't even trying. You gave me someone to talk to. And that's really the best thing even if I did all the saving." Even when in pain, Cooper is smiling. He ceases to amaze me.

"I never saved you. I never gave you someone to talk to. I talked about myself and I should have asked about you. I should have made you talk about yourself."

"Lorraine, shut up. Dammit, Lorraine. I love you, I'm in love with you. And I don't regret a thing because you gave me the best four days of my life. Holy crap, Lorraine. If I could kiss you right now without making you disgusted, I would kiss you."

"Cooper, don't you dare leave me now. Fight for me, damnit." I cry harder because I am trying to comprehend a world without Cooper Allen Ross. CAR, the guy who just told me he's in love with me.

"I'm not leaving you, I promise." He says brushing my hair away even though he must be really weak. Ambulances start to pull up a few minutes later. Cooper just stares up at me with blank eyes.

"Cooper, come on. The ambulances are here." I smile at him because he promised me and I'm holding him to the promise.

"Cooper." I smile, shaking him.

"Come on, Cooper. Wake up. Surprise me with those greenish eyes and make my dreams come true. Wake up. Please." I whisper, shaking him while my voice thickens and cracks.

"We have an unresponsive young male, let's revive him." One man in a medical uniform said as two people brought paddles over and placed them on his chest.

"No! Cooper! Wake up! He's going to wake up, don't worry! He promised me!" I cry as two men pull me away from Cooper's lifeless body. I watched as they received failed attempts to wake Cooper up. I know before the man walks over to me that Cooper is dead. He is gone. The man didn't need to tell me that, but he did and he places a hand on my shoulder in sympathy. I don't cry. I just stare straight ahead in fear that if I start crying, it would make it real.

"We need to check your arm and see if you are okay. Can we do that?" The man asks me before I nod and follow him to the back of the ambulance where they check my head and my arm. The arm wound I had received from the other night was pretty bad and deep, but I didn't think anything of it. In fact, I hadn't even really noticed it until a police officer pointed it out to one of the nurses that was on the scene. I told them I am fine but they said that I would need to ride to the hospital with them and receive stitches. I agree and hug Cooper before I leave.

"I'm sorry you didn't get your dream to create your own art. You deserve it more than I deserve a second chance. You know I love you, Coop. Damn it, am I in love with you and I'm sorry I didn't tell you. I couldn't stop thinking about you every day. I'll make you proud and I'll take care of Linda and your dad, I promise." I kiss him on the lips and whisper, "I wish I could've done that before you left me for good. And I didn't think it was disgusting."

As I ride in the back of the ambulance away from Cooper, all that is in my head is all the things he said and did over the week. I pull out my phone, played, "*Please Don't Go,*" by Joel Adams, and cry silently into my hands.

****

When I get to the hospital, the doctors stitch up my arm. I don't pay attention to anything they say or do to me; I'm completely numb in all of my senses.

"Is there anybody we can call for you?" A nurse asks me, sympathetically.

"No. I'm just going to go when you guys let me. I'll-I can make it home."

"Well you're free to go." The nurse speaks again, looking at me with uncertainty.

"Thank you." I say before walking out of the hospital doors and breathing in the cold air that Cooper had breathed in once but now, he no longer breathes at all.

"Why'd you leave me?" I whisper into the air as if Cooper can actually hear me. I walk toward the bar where it all happened.

****

The bell of the bar dings, signaling someone walking into the bar; it was me.

"I'm sorry we are—Lorraine." Linda says coming out of the shadows.

"Where the hell did you go? I was worried sick about you." She says, putting her hands on her hips and wrapping her cardigan around herself.

"I went to go see Cooper. Your ex had found him too." I say, walking behind the bar, towards the alcohol.

"Where is he? Is Cooper okay? Is he hurt?" She asks, walking closer to me, demanding information.

"I don't know, Linda. What the hell did you do to this guy that makes him want to hurt us so badly? He said that you did the same thing to him. Did you hurt his family? Did you kill someone?" I ask her grabbing a beer from the fridge, the same beer company that I had opened my first bottle of beer. The same company that I drank with Cooper. I threw the bottle of beer against the wall.

"This is all your fault." I scream, wondering if I was screaming at Linda for causing this or screaming at myself for watching Cooper die and not doing anything about it.

"What happened, Lorraine?" She asks still clueless, but I bet she had an idea.

"You went to prison for murder, didn't you? You just told everybody it was fraud but it was murder. You killed your husband's family, right?" I ask her, breathless.

"Yes, alright! I went to jail for murder. I killed my husband's son and his girlfriend. Not a day goes by that I don't hate myself for it everyday. I don't need people knowing and reminding me of it. Now what happened to Cooper?" She asks me, throwing her rag that was on her shoulder on the floor.

"Well put the pieces together, Linda. If I didn't die and he came for revenge, who do you think he killed?" I ask my lip quivering.

"No." She whispers, hands over her mouth.

"He's dead." I cry before exiting the bar and running all the way home.

****

When I walk in my house, I didn't think my mom would even still be up. But she is. And she is crying.

"Mom, are you okay?" I ask sitting down beside her, even though she has no idea what I had been through just now.

"Lorraine." She says hugging me, clutching my hand.

"Are you okay, Mom?" I ask again, moving my seat closer to her so that I could put my arm around her shoulders.

"I got a call from your father's lawyer. He isn't coming home because he's going to jail. He said that he killed someone. I can't believe it." My mom says crying even harder.

"It's okay, Mom. I'm sure, Dad didn't kill anybody. Everything's going to work out. I promise." I say to her as she sucks up her tears and smiles. I wasn't phased by this because Cooper's death was still so fresh in my mind.

"I'm sure it'll work out, too." She says, kissing my cheek and shooing me of to bed. I wouldn't be surprised if my father was accused for murder, to be honest. I pull out my laptop and write for a while. I didn't know what the hell I was actually writing about until my fingers stopped moving and my mind actually caught up with my hands. After posting it and closing my laptop, I cry myself to sleep, knowing that in the morning, I won't be able to meet Cooper at the bar.

****

ENTRY:

When I walked out of my room this morning, I didn't know what the day held. I knew that something good and something bad was going to happen today, but I didn't know I would actually lose someone that I cared about a lot. It's when you least expect it that someone leaves your life. Sometimes, you can see that something is going to happen. Someone is going to leave your life, but sometimes it's slow. For the people around you, it's bad and good. It gives you time to morn and say goodbye. But its bad for the person that is in pain and hurting. A quick death, like a knife to the heart or a shot to the head is horrible for the people who love you and adore you. But, it's better for the person who is dying though, because you don't experience as much pain and heartache.

Today, I lost the one man that showed me what pure kindness is; the stranger who opened his heart and allowed one more person in before he lost his life saving mine. He saved my life physically and emotionally, even though I knew him only for such a short while. Cooper showed me valuable things that I will carry over into a different life.

If I could go back and say the things that I should've said, I would. I would've said countless, "I'm in love with you"s because I mean it. I would say he looked handsome in his work uniform. I would visit him at school and go get ice cream with him and take long walks with him in the park. I would spend all of the time

I had with Cooper Allen Ross. If I could bring him back so I could have one more good day with him, I would.

We had less than a week to get to know each other, but we did. We did all of the things that it would take other people months to do. It took us a little more than three days to exchange numbers and information, but most importantly, in this short time I learned to trust Cooper Allen Ross; my best friend. He knew more about me than my own family does. He knew more about me than I do.

Cooper still stayed by me until his last breath because he said I was worth dying for. From his name that flowed so perfectly together, to his eyes that were as green as a golf course on a hot summer day. To his smile that made all the girls fall to their knees; I loved it all. In fact, I still love it. I love every single thing about him. He knew I fell in love with him. Because he fell in love with me too. But we just went along and pretended like nothing happened. But I knew that someday we would be together. I just had no idea I would lose him so early and never get my chance.

When I met Cooper, I was a girl who had just got her heart broken and didn't think that there was any hope. I mean no hope at all. But Cooper changed everything for me and he healed me. I thought that there would be scars left on my heart from my ex-boyfriend, but there isn't. There was just Cooper, and the way he made me feel. He saved me in more ways than I've ever been saved. Heaven gained an angel today. Cooper Allen Ross will always hold my heart even if he isn't here to know it.

****

CHAPTER 4:

THREE DAYS LATER...

When I wake up, I wake up to a pounding pain in my heart. The pain of loss. It was the same every morning. I get up and walk downstairs. My mother is making breakfast with a glum look on her face while my brother is sitting down at the table.

"Good morning, Mom. Hey, buddy." I say, rubbing Johnny's hair.

"Mom's making breakfast and then she said we are going to go out for ice cream or something." John says making eye contact with Mom. Something is wrong but I am not going to butt in and say something about it, for I am too weak and too tired to associate a long conversation with anybody.

"Okay." I say putting my head down on the table and going to sleep.

****

"Lorraine, wake up." My mom shakes me awake.

"I'm awake!" I jolt up, mumbling.

"Are you feeling alright, Lorraine?" My brother asks, staring cautiously over at me while shoving pancakes into his mouth.

"Yeah, I'm fine." I say, taking the pancakes from my mother and using my fork to dig them around the plate. I am not hungry. I didn't even want to think about food for the fear I might throw up whatever is even still in my stomach.

"Eat up." My brother watches me as I watch the pancakes that suffer my fork like I suffer the loss of Cooper. I am seeing everything as if it is dead. With Cooper, I would see everything in such a crisp and bright way. Now, I am back to what I used to be. For my brother's sake, I take a bite of the pancakes that look destroyed.

"Alright, Lorraine. Go get changed and meet us in the car." My mother says, before grabbing her keys and my brother. She glances at me before she leaves the house. I throw out the pancakes and put the dish in the sink. After washing my hands of the syrup that was on the pancakes, I walk slowly upstairs and change into a pair of sweats and a white t-shirt from my dad's closet.

When I grab my phone, that's when I see it. The picture that Cooper drew for me with the note he gave me. I unpin it from my wall and take it with me. Even if it's a big laminated piece of paper and a small little note. I take them with me and hold them close to my chest. I hold them close to my heart, just like I hold Cooper.

****

As we are driving, which worries me a bit because of my mother's condition, she asks, "What is in your hands?"

"A picture." I look out the window. As we stop at a red light, my mother asks, "Can I see it?"

I hand it over to her and keep the note with me.

"It's beautiful. I'm guessing it's supposed to be you. Who drew it?" She asks, looking over to see the pained expression on my face.

"Someone who was once very close to me. He's gone though." I lay my head against the seatbelt.

"What do you mean he's gone?" She asks me, pressing on the gas as the light went green. Like Cooper's eyes.

"He died." I watch the stoplight disappear behind us. A tear slips down my face as I think of the green light that forced my mom to go. Just like the green light in Cooper's eyes faded when the man forced him to go.

****

"Where are we?" I ask my mom, watching her face sink.

"Dr. Joanne Nova. She's a—"

"Psychiatrist." I point to a sign in the front of the building.

"Look, I just want you to see her for one session. I just want you to—"

"I know what a psychiatrist is, Mom! I don't want to see one." I cross my arms and hold Cooper's picture close to my heart.

"Honey, I know losing Cooper was hard—"

"What did you just say?" I ask her.

"I know losing—" And then she realized her mistake.

"HOW THE FREAKING HELL DO YOU KNOW ABOUT COOPER!" I scream at her, my eyes starting to produce tears.

"ANN1295." She says, staring at my face, her eyebrows scrunched up in discomfort.

"That was you?" I ask breathlessly.

"I'm sorry, honey. But your blogs were really good. I wanted to—"

"You can't just do that to me, Mom! You can't do any of this to me!" I yell, getting out of the car and walking into the parking lot.

"Johnny, lock the doors." My mom says before getting out of the car and following me, even though I have no idea where the hell I am going.

"Lorraine!" My mother calls out. I pause for a second.

"Why are you doing this to me? Why are you making this so much harder for me to go through?" I ask her, throwing my hands up in the air.

"I'm just trying to help you, Lorraine. Let me help you." She walks closer to me.

"I let Cooper help me. When he fixed me, I felt like a million bucks. I felt as if I could fly, even though I've never been on a plane before. When we were together, I knew what the phrase, "meant to be," felt like. I felt like I belonged there in that moment, I felt like I belonged to him and all his problems, I felt like I belonged with him.

"Now I know that I was *meant to be* with him, not as a friend, but as my love. He knew me better than I know myself and I only knew him for four days. Okay? Four days and he knew me better than I know myself. Don't try to fix me because Cooper is the only one who can fix me right now, but he's gone." I walk into the building where Dr. Joanne Nova is. I am going to go through this even if it meant recalling the feelings that I had felt when Cooper left me. Not for my mother, but for my brother who is staring at me right now as if I am a lost person.

****

"Hi, I'm looking for a Doctor Nova?" I ask the front desk of the building, clutching the only thing that I had left to remind me of Cooper.

"Third floor, Room 124." She says, directing me towards the elevator to the right.

"Thank you." I say before entering the elevator and pressing the button with the number three.

After getting out of the elevator, the Room 124 is the first door on the left. I open it slowly and there is a waiting room there. A couple of chairs are against the wall, some playing toys for little kids are in the corner and magazines line the wall, their pages probably read a hundred times by adults. It is a nice little room for people to hang out but it was very silent. The silence made me anxious.

After a couple of minutes of staring at one specific spot on the wall to calm my anxiety, a beautiful woman with a dark pixie cut in a slick pencil skirt with a white blouse and a black cardigan came out of a room, opposite side from the one I came from.

"Miss Lorraine Lowry?" She calls out, her voice being more perfect than anything I have heard in a while.

I stood up and took a good look at her. She is beautiful. She isn't the beautiful that you see on the streets every day or have waking up beside you. She is a genuinely beautiful person, and I bet under all the makeup she is wearing, she is too.

"Lorraine Lowry." I hold out my hand to her.

"Joanne Nova." I like how she doesn't say Doctor before her name. I like how it seems she wants to become my friend before my doctor.

She steps back and allows me to walk into her office. She shuts the door behind me and gestures to the stereotypical couch in the corner of the room. The office is a well-spaced out room, and she has photos lining the walls filled with adventures that she must've been on.

"Wow." I say as her photos took my breath away with every one.

"Where did you go?" I ask marveled by her traveling.

"I went everywhere you can imagine. I went from Hawaii to Brazil to California. I traveled all over the place with my best friend." She said clasping her hands behind her back, clearly uncomfortable.

"What happened to your best friend? Is she still your best friend?" I ask her even though I was here to talk about me.

"I'm sorry. I don't mean to pry." I look at her.

"No, you're fine. I lost my best friend but we are here for you." She takes a seat at her desk and folds her hands.

"We are going to have to do some digging. So what are some things that are concerning you?" I fold my hands and place them behind my head, laying down.

"I lost my best friend to murder." I release a breath I didn't know I was holding in.

"Wow. Okay, that was very-"

"Abrupt?" I ask her, knowing I was very front.

"No. I just wasn't expecting that. But I know how it feels. I lost my best friend to the same thing." She offers me an encouraging smile.

"I've only known him for a short period but we had a really special connection and I lost him couple of nights ago. Someone was coming after us because his mother did some pretty terrible things and instead of killing me, Cooper saved me and was killed instead." I glance over at Dr. Nova.

"How do you feel with him gone?" Joanne asks, searching for an emotion she can probably work with to make me feel better.

"Lost. Like there is no hope. And I'm feeling pretty lonely without him."

"Did you have any feelings regarding love towards your friend, Cooper?" She asks me.

"Yes. Now that I think about it, I loved him more than I love a friend. But I only have a picture that he drew me. It's all I have to remember him by." I hold the picture out to her.

"He was an excellent artist. And I bet he was a pretty amazing friend if he was to write this note to you and draw you like he did." She says holding the note. I hadn't realized that I had let her take the note, too. I remember exactly what he wrote.

You told me to draw you. So I drew you from my point of view.

XOXO,

Cooper.

"He was." I say, taking the picture and the note back.

"What do you think Cooper would feel right now if he was looking down at you?"

"I think he would be mad at me for being like this and he would want me to be happy and remember him forever. He would want me to live my life." I think of Cooper looking down on me right now in Dr. Nova's office.

"You should do whatever you think Cooper would want you to do. You should do what you think Cooper would want you to do because Cooper is the way to your heart. Follow Cooper; follow your heart. Just like Cooper saved you that one time, he is going to save you again.

"Whenever you feel sad, I want you to think of how Cooper would want you to feel and what he would want you to do. Do you think you understand what I am trying to say?" She asks me.

I nod and smile. "Cooper always wanted to become an artist. But he never had enough money to pay for college."

"I would've paid for whatever he needed." I say, my eyes clouding up with tears.

"I bet he was really grateful for that." She stands up and leans against the wall.

"He never knew about it. I only told his step-mother." I push away the tears that were yet to fall.

"I bet he would have been grateful for that, Lorraine. If he was anything like a true friend which I'm pretty sure he was, he would have been grateful for everything you did for him. Is that the only thing that is bothering you?" She asks me sitting down on the edge of the desk, in front of me.

"Actually, no. My mother claims that she got a call from my father last night and he killed someone. He's going to go through a trial now but I just don't know how to feel about something like that. I mean he was never there for me anyways but he was still my father, you know? And I still love him. But what he did is so unforgivable, if he actually did do what he claims he did. And I don't know if this even happened. I've learned in the past not to really trust my mother too much, she usually lets me down eventually.

"She claims that we need to all work together but it's really herself who needs to work harder for all of us. My brother and I have been working harder than anybody even realizes just to stay afloat. I mean we have a lot of money, but that's not the point."

"Well I wouldn't worry too much about your mother, if those are the only things that are troubling you about her, but just be on the look out for information about your father. I have a feeling your mother is telling the truth so make sure you keep a close eye on that. Anything else?" Dr. Nova asks me.

"This all started because of one simple heartbreak. One simple, now meaningless, heartbreak. I don't know if whether I could've prevented it or stopped it, but it happened and now Cooper is dead, my mother is paranoid and lonely, my father is going to jail, my brother is clueless and desperate for attention, and I am still broken and lost." I sigh, moving my attention to the pictures on the wall.

"I wish I could travel with Cooper. I would give anything to have one more day with him."

"You couldn't have done anything to change the circumstances. You couldn't have done anything to change what is and what happened. It's in the past. I bet Cooper wouldn't want you to keep dragging his death on. He would want you to be happy with your life and move on." She says, standing up.

"I will never move on. It's something that happened. Moving on is forgetting. He's too important to forget. He was the one that was stabbed and I feel as though I was stabbed too." I say, sitting up and slouching on purpose.

"Moving on isn't forgetting. It's knowing that someone is gone and not breaking down into tears as soon as their name is mentioned. Moving on is letting go but not of the memories you share. Not of all the feelings, just letting go of the idea of him because you are hurting. Moving on lets the other person move on too. Right now, Cooper needs you to move on." Dr. Nova says adjusting the things on her desk.

"How did you move on?" I ask her curiously. "I don't mean to pry again, I just think it's better to know someone else's story."

"I didn't. I...sunk into something doctors call depression. But I eventually was helped by a doctor to learn how to deal with depression and then I found out I wanted to help people emotionally, too." She says, sighing before smiling at me.

"So what do you think is keeping you from letting go of the poster in your arms?"

I look down and see that I am clutching onto the poster of me that Cooper had drew for me.

"The fact that every time I think of Cooper, I am going to have to say I 'used' to know him because he's dead now. We were going to go on a road trip to look at colleges. Guess that's another thing I am going to have to say goodbye to." I say, glancing up at her as she writes it down on a piece of notepad paper she has on her desk.

"Let's say it was the other way around and a couple of nights ago, you died instead of Cooper. How would you want him to react to your death?" She says, using a different way of looking at things.

"I would want him to cry for a bit but then I wouldn't want him to live his life going through depression." I say, thinking about how things would be different if I had been the one to die.

"How do you think he would react?" She tilts her head to the side and watches the expression on my face.

"I think he would sink into depression." I clutch my lip in pain. I try as hard as I could to contain the tears that were about to flow like a flood from the clouds.

"It's alright to cry, Lorraine. People cry for days straight and when they aren't crying, they are staring at a blank wall, at nothingness." She gets up to sit down next to me.

"It's so hard. I never thought losing someone could be so hard." I say, feeling a huge bubble in my throat from the strength I am using to hold back the tears in my eyes.

"It's always hard to lose someone. But, when it is someone you truly care about and know, it's just that much harder to make it through their death. I know it's hard right now, especially since his death was a couple of days ago, but I know that this is just the beginning of something really hard you are going to have to pull yourself through. Some people might not understand but I want you to know that

I understand." She says, putting an arm around my shoulders.

"Do you think that it would have been better if you followed something that you wouldn't have liked but would have made you a lot of money?" I ask her, moving my head to look at her. Her arm drifts off my shoulder to rest beside her.

"I don't focus on the 'what-if's anymore. There are too many 'what-if's in life to focus on. You just have to live with all the decisions you make that you believe are right instead of thinking about what could've been or what could be." She says, standing up and holding out her hands for me to get up too. I take her hands and she helps me to get up off of her comfortable couch.

"I want you to shut your eyes and think of the things that scare you the most." She watches my facial expressions. I shut my eyes tight and receive flashbacks from the moment in the alleyway of the familiar man that stabbed Cooper.

Then, my brain plays back the moment when I found out Cooper was actually dead and how that could've been me. In a way, it was me. Part of me died when Cooper died. The part that he saved. My brother at the table this morning scared me. I am scared that he would have to mature early, just like me, and learn by himself because his sister would be stuck in depression and so would our mother, who is starting to slowly sink without my father. It is time to finally step up and help the family once again.

"I'm scared of the man coming after me again. I'm scared that my mother is slipping into depression again and I'm scared that my brother will have to grow up without a good role model." I spit out quicker than I can think it through.

"Here is my card. If you think you are in danger, I want you to call me. I'll come with help. My brother was a police officer and still has a gun. As for your mother, though it's a lot of responsibility, I want you to try to help her the best you can. How are you scared that your brother will grow up without a role model if you are there? Set a good example. Work hard for what you want and show him that through everything you've been through, you are standing tall and ready to fight for what you believe in. Show him that you believe in him." She says, sighing.

"Thank you." I take the card from her and slip it into my pocket. I grab the picture, the one Cooper drew for me, and stand next to Dr. Nova.

"I'm better at listening than sharing. So if you ever need me," I hold out a little piece of paper with my phone number on it.

"Thank you." Dr. Nova says, smiling brightly.

"Well you helped me so I feel like I have to pay you back."
I smile at her. It feels good to smile. I feel relieved in a
way to have talked to someone about everything.

"You know I really didn't want to come in here. Now I'm
glad I did." I smile again because it feels great.

"Talking to someone puts you in a good mood. Talk to
your brother. Let him talk and listen." She puts a hand on
my shoulder.

"I will. Thank you." I say, pulling out the card and
nodding, before slipping it back into my pocket and
opening the door.

"Oh, Lorraine, wait. You forgot this." She says, picking up
my note and handing it to me before I left the room.

"Thank you." I smile again brightly before leaving the room with a smile on my face. I enter the elevator with a bright smile on my face. I think this was going to be my turn for the better.

****

"Hey, guys." I smile at my family and wave as my mom opens the car. I really see the bags under her eyes now and how much hurt is on her face that she is trying to hide. She is fighting herself, trying to make it better for my brother and I.

"Hi, sweetie. How did it go?" She asks me, smiling because she sees the smile on my face.

"Good, good. Mom, why don't you let me drive?" I ask her, getting out of the front seat without an answer from my mother.

"Okay, if you want to." She says, before getting out and leaving the door open. She wraps her arms around me and whispers in my ear, "Thank you for going. It means a lot to me."

"I actually enjoyed it." I whisper back, kissing her cheek. I watch as my mother lets go of me and with a smile even though the bags under her eyes beg to differ, enters the passenger side of the front seat.

With a car full of smiles and happy music, I pull out of the garage where I met Dr. Joanne Nova.

****

"Mom, I'm going to go out for a little bit. Is that okay?" I ask her, watching her facial expressions.

"That's fine, sweetie. Just be home before dark." She says, knowing that I won't be home for a while.

"I'll be home way before then." I smile before rubbing my brother's head with my hand as he squeals. I laugh and exit my house. Getting into the car, I turned on the radio and headed for Linda.

****

The bells in the front from the door go off as I notice the open sign in the front window but no customers in the bar.

"Welcome to Billy's Bar. How can I—" She walks out from behind the wall, rubbing her eyes.

"Linda." I say, watching her face. Now that I take a good look, I could see the wrinkles and the worn out expression in her eyes. Her makeup was running down her face but she tried to wipe away the gray tinted tears.

"What are you doing here?" She asks me her voice hoarse as she sits down at the bar.

"I came to see you." I say moving to sit down next to her.

"Don't." She gets up and moves towards the wall.

"Linda, what's the matter?" I ask her, trying to get through to her.

"Cooper's dead." She yells, as though I didn't know he wasn't breathing anymore.

"I know, Linda, but you can't keep doing this. I've come to see you every day since it happened and each day you are worse than the other. You know what doctors call this? Sinking into depression. It's over. He's gone. You need to move on from this. Okay? It's over. He's gone." I say, looking at her. For the first time, I don't cry when mentioning Cooper.

"It's all my fault." She says, putting her hands over her eyes.

"It doesn't get any better if you keep beating yourself up over it. It was all that man's fault, so stop this. Please. For Cooper." I ask her, moving closer.

She wipes her eyes and smiles at me before putting her arms around me.

"Since when did you get so strong and brave?" She asks, hugging me close.

"Since now. I promise that it'll get better with time. We will learn to deal with this. But crying over it isn't going to bring him back." I release her as she releases me. She nods before smiling again.

"I think we are starting to recover." She says, combing through her hair.

"Who is 'we?'" I ask her, curiously.

"Her and I." A man comes out from behind the wall, sounding familiar.

"Cooper." I whisper seeing the man that I had lost three days ago.

****

"Cooper was my son." He says, sounding exactly like Cooper.

"But you sound so much like him. You look so much like him." I say, moving closer to him as if stuck in a trance.

"Russell Ross, Cooper's father." He holds out his hand. I shake it with a certain uneasiness about the way he is acting. He is perfectly fine with Cooper being gone. He doesn't blame Linda or anything by the looks of it.

"Pleasure to finally meet the man who gave Cooper nothing." I spit at him and walk away.

"Pleasure to meet you too, Miss Lorraine." My head snaps around as I walk away and I turn towards him slowly.

"How the hell do you know my name?" I slither at him as if I was a snake.

"Do you think I was that bad of a father that I didn't know who my son was hanging out with?" He asks, laughing.

"I do think you were a bad father for Cooper. He didn't get anything from you. All he got was bad mentalities and lessons that he wanted to teach to his future kids that he never got to create." I say, putting my hand on my hip and watching Cooper's father not even get uncomfortable.

"I'm surprised my son didn't do the deed and impregnate you, slut." He spits at me, smiling.

"Russell!" Linda shouts at her husband. I hate name-calling. Especially if it's the word, "slut." It's vile and poisonous, and I wish I could take it out of people's words towards me. It just makes me feel worse about myself.

"Don't worry, Linda. I can handle another horrible father." I eye Russell with my crystal eyes that turned to a black because of the darkness that was coming off of Russell.

"I loved your son. Even though you are a prick, he was an amazing person. Better than anything he learned from you. Linda is a better role model and she has blood all over her hands." I spit at him and then realize my mistake.

He had no idea what Linda had done in the past. I don't watch Linda's reaction to my sudden burst of confidence. I just exit the bar and listen to the yelling that comes out of it. After sitting on the steps for an hour or two, Linda steps out with a tear streaked face and a no-makeup face, different from before. Silence stays in the air as the wind hits us both in the face. I speak up first, "I'm so sorry."

I stare ahead as Linda says, "It's alright. I was due to tell him sooner or later."

"I'm still sorry." I say, turning to watch her face.

"It's seriously okay." She says, smiling light at me.

"So what happens now?" I ask, after a couple of beats of silence.

"I don't know. I guess we try to move on with our lives." She says, shrugging.

"Those days with Cooper were the best days of my life." I smile, wincing when I feel the pain again in my heart.

"They always are. All around, he was really a wonderful person." She says thinking of Cooper with a smile on her face now.

"Yea." I say as she hugs me. I hug her back before releasing her and leaning my head against her shoulder.

"I'm going to miss coming in to sit in that corner booth and having Cooper bring me my coffee." I tear up at the thought of never getting my coffee from Cooper again.

"I'm going to miss him being rude to me." She says, lightly laughing. I laugh along with her until my vision gets blurred with tears.

"He really cared for you, I hope you know that." I let Linda know in case she didn't. She nods and smiles.

"He knew you for less than a week and he cared for you like nobody else. The way he looked at you, you could tell he was in love with you, deeply." She says looking sideways at me.

"Thank you." I whisper my voice thickening.

"For what? You did everything by yourself." She says, smiling at me while she watches my eyes water up.

"I can't believe only a couple of days ago, I walked into this little diner and sat at the corner booth while I thought Cooper was risking his job for me but he was really just willing to sit down and listen to a stranger talk about her problems." I laugh at the thought that Cooper couldn't actually get fired opposite to what I thought. Linda joins in laughing with me as I keep my head on her shoulder and stare straight ahead at the little flower shop across the street because I am afraid of what would come if I turn my head to stare at the alleyway where I had lost it all.

****

"LORRAINE!!! HELP ME!!!" Cooper screams.

"Cooper, where are you?" I ask, wanting to know where the screaming was coming from so I could save him.

"LORRAINE!!! HELP M—" And then the screaming got silent. When I turned the corner, Cooper was sprawled out dead with a dagger in his side and his eyes wide open, staring at me. I run over to Cooper.

"NO!" I scream, tears falling down my face like the rain that was suddenly pouring over my head.

"COOPER!" I scream.

"COOPER!" I scream.

"COOPER!"

"HE'S DEAD, LORRAINE!" Someone screams in my face. My eyes suddenly open and I stare at Linda.

"Where am I?" I ask embarrassed by my screaming and my nightmare.

"You fell asleep on my shoulder so I moved you into the bar." She says, holding my shoulder, clearly defeated.

"Oh." I say before standing up and getting a bit dizzy.

"Take your time." She says letting go of my shoulder to hand me a cup of water. I gulp it down, in need for some hydration.

"Thank you." I say before taking a deep breath. I hand her back the now empty glass and walk towards the door.

"Where do you think you are going?" Linda asks hand on hip.

"I promised my mom I would be home before dark. I intend to keep my promise. I'll see you tomorrow." I say before walking out the door and leaving behind Linda and her ridiculous husband, Russell.

****

"Mom?" I whisper, shaking her shoulder. When I walked into the house, my mother was passed out on the dinning room table, head in hands while my brother was eating dinner next to her.

"Huh?" She wakes up muttering and looking around with only half of her eyes open.

"Mom, it's Lorraine. I want you to go upstairs and go to bed. Okay? I've got everything else under control. Go up to bed." I say before helping her up. Once she got up the stairs safely, I sat down in the seat my mother was sleeping in.

"Hey, bud. How was your day?" I ask him curiously, trying to make conversation.

"Same as the last, lonely and boring." He says, pushing at his eggs.

"Since when did you learn to make eggs?" I ask him, smiling, trying to bring up the mood and not make it take a downfall.

"Since I had to learn how to make it on my own." Johnny says staring at his disgusting-looking eggs.

"Hey, bud, what's the matter?" I ask him putting a hand on his shoulder. All of a sudden, he just jumps out of his seat, cuddles in my lap, and starts to cry. I wrap my arms tightly around the 5-year-old who was going through more than he was equipped to handle at an age like his.

"It's okay, Johnny. It will get better, I promise. I'm going to make it better, little squish." I say calling him the name I gave him when he first came out of the womb. I hold Johnny until he falls asleep. Then I wrap his legs around my waist and hold him with one hand while I shut the lights off, lock the doors, and walk up the stairs. I put the alarm on and tuck Johnny into bed before washing my face and slipping into a deep sleep.

****

When I wake up to the alarm, my brain switches into gear. I grab the bat that I always kept my bed and open my bedroom door. The hallways were clear. I slowly walk down the stairs, carefully not to make any noise. I check the bathroom before walking into the dining room. A man is going through the fridge. I turn on the lights and say, "Step away from the fridge or I'll knock you out." The man backs away from the fridge with his hands up.

"Dad?" I ask, before the man takes his familiar and scary clown mask off and true enough, my dad is standing in his kitchen late at night going through his own fridge.

"What the hell are you doing here?" I ask him, shutting off the alarm. He sits down at the table and stares at me.

"What?" I ask him, looking down at me to see if I have a stain or something.

"I never realized how beautiful you were." He says rubbing his white head of hair. I roll my eyes with a laugh lodged in my throat.

"Dad, this is no time for compliments. And stop trying to change the subject. Talk." I say, sitting down at the other end of the table with the bat ready under my legs. If what Mom said is true, I should have the bat ready.

"Look, I know this is going to be quick and hard for you to hear but you have to hear it. Okay?" He asks me, whispering.

"Why are you whispering?" I ask him.

"Because I have a feeling we aren't alone." He says, searching the room for another human but no other person in the room.

"Mom's up?" I mouth not making a sound.

"No. Johnny." He mouths back, no sound coming out of his mouth.

"What do you have to tell me?" I ask him, not making a sound.

"I'm going to prison," He mouths before saying out loud, "I want you to visit me."

"Why? Didn't they hold your trial?" I ask him.

"I was guilty. I thought I told your mother. I just need you to visit me. Can you do that?" He asks, staring into my crystal blue eyes that were lost.

"Okay. I guess. When?" I ask him.

"Tomorrow. 3 o'clock sharp." He says, before leaving the front door. I didn't get an "I love you" or a "I missed you." I get a "visit me in prison." I try to turn the alarm back on but it wouldn't go on so I leave it off.

I climb the stairs and peak into Johnny's room before I put my head on my pillow again. The ironic part is that Johnny is sound asleep, his breathing right. When I peak into my Mom's room, she is nowhere to be found and the window is open. I run back down the stairs and peak out the window.

My mother is standing beside my father having a deep conversation. I watch their actions as my mother hit my father across the face and my father kisses my mother before disappearing into the shadows. I moved towards the kitchen table. I sit down and wait for my mother to come in. When she did, she sat beside me and explained to me that my father had murdered for payback. After listening to my mother's non-sense, I walk with her upstairs to our separate bedrooms. As soon as my head hit the bed, darkness falls over me and I slept well for the first time in a while.

****

THE NEXT DAY @ 3:

I stand inside the prison waiting room and allow my nerves to calm before seeing my father in an orange jumpsuit and that same smug look on his face. As the officer leads me into a room just like the ones in the movies, I sit down and wait for my father to appear in the window in front of me. As the door opens, my father walks in just the way I pictured him all this morning. He sits in front of me, the only thing keeping us apart this piece of plastic. I pick up the telephone just as he picks up his so we can speak to each other.

"Lorraine, I'm so glad you came."

"Well, I said I was going to come, didn't I?"

"You must be wondering why I asked you to meet me here." He says, smiling.

"Yeah, I might be a little curious."

"I want you to know what happened and why I am in here." He says, looking into my eyes, the smile on his face gone, now replaced with the look of evil.

"Why are you in here, Dad?" I ask him nervous about the answer I was going to receive.

"A long time ago, I was married to a different woman. We married for the money and for the company. Though the whole reason we got a divorce was because of her and her *wonderful* company. I had three adoptive children before I physically had you and your brother. They were foster kids and my wife and I had really wanted kids so we adopted. The children started to grow up and then one day, my wife murdered our adoptive son and his girlfriend. I was devastated and she left the house even though it was obvious that I kicked her out already. The last thing I told her was that I would get revenge.

"I wasn't a good single parent so I left the little girl and her big brother alone. I regret it everyday of my life but after everything that's happened now, I have a lot to regret." He says with a smirk, making chills run up my spine.

"After Linda killed my favorite son, I was saddened. One day, a woman walked into my life, your mother, and she healed all my wounds. We were really meant to be, everybody could tell. We got married, had you two and then we kept it steady. Everything was going perfect.

"Then I saw Linda one day in the market. I followed her to her stupid bar and saw her son. He was handsome and everything that I saw for Anderson, our foster child. He was going to make it big in the NBA. I never saw our children again but I know they must have turned out wonderful because of the way I raised them. A couple of days ago, I got revenge on her. Though I know you must probably already think I'm a horrible person, I murdered her son. His girlfriend, I couldn't get to her so I just let her be. But I saw how it affected Linda and now I feel relieved." He sighs and looks at me. I had tears running down my face and I felt my face getting red but he didn't seem to care.

"What was her son's name?" I ask my stranger-of-a-father who right now isn't even my father for killing a familiar boy. He isn't a stranger. He's farther away than a stranger.

"I'm not sure. I think it was something with a C in front and it rhymed with poop." My father says shaking his head.

I break down, crying. "Coop." I whisper, lightly.

"Oh, you knew him?" Steve Lowry asks me.

"You *asshole*. It all makes sense now. I was wondering why you were so familiar. You don't remember me, do you, Dad? You don't remember hitting me in the head with the back of a knife? You don't remember almost stabbing me but *killing my best friend* instead? You don't remember telling me that Linda did the same thing to you? You don't remember killing my best friend?" I yell at the stranger before me named Steve Lowry, my *supposed* dad.

"That was you?" My father asks, staring at me with wide eyes. I just stare back at him because I can't bring myself to say that I was the one who was tied up in a chair and almost killed in an alleyway.

"You killed him." I sob, trying to bring myself to stop crying but I can't. My father killed my best friend. And it's all my fault.

"I didn't even know that was you." He says wide-eyed. He doesn't apologize; he just stares.

"Doesn't make it right." I say, wiping away my tears that had ruined my makeup.

"Do you know when I was little, I used to think you were my hero? That you were like the Superman to the world?

But you never saved me. You saved everybody else but your own daughter.

"Instead of being the Superman you were when I was little, you were the Lex Luther and you killed my best friend." I say, putting my head down in shame. It was my fault that Cooper died.

"It doesn't matter now, he's gone. So just suck it up and move on with your life." He says without so much as a blink.

"What did you just say?" I ask, watching his facial expressions in disgust.

"I said, it—" I slam my hand hard on the plastic between us.

"Don't you *dare* say that to me *again*. Cooper taught me more than you ever did my whole life. Don't give me *shit* about how *I* need to move on from Cooper. He was the best *damn* thing that ever happened to me." I say, covering my mouth, trying to hide the loud sobs coming out of my throat.

"Lorraine—"

"Don't even say my name. You don't deserve it. You deserve this." I say, gesturing towards the prison and its inmates.

"Come visit me again when you cool down." My father says waving me off with his hand, a devilish smirk on his face. I hope he enjoyed his life sentence, or at least that's what I hoped it was.

"Never will I ever come here again. I'll make sure you are *never* in my life again. Not in my *children's*, not in my *husband's*, not in *Johnny's*, and sure as *hell* not in my *mother's*." I say, before slamming the telephone down and walking out the room where my father confessed to me the biggest shock of my life. It couldn't get any worse than this.

****

"LINDA!" I scream searching for her behind the bar and in her rooms.

"LINDA!" I scream again hoping that she is here even though there was a closed sign on the door.

"She's not here." Russell says, coming out of the shadows.

"I need to talk to Linda." I sob, wobbling.

"Hey, hey. It's okay. You'll be okay." Russell says, catching me in his arms.

"I can't—It's my fault he's gone. It's all my fault." I sob into Russell's chest.

Russell was so tall, that I had to look up to him. When I fell into his arms, I was only up to his chest. My head just skimmed his shoulder.

"No it's not. Don't you dare say that. If he cared about anyone, it would be you. He wouldn't stop talking about you but he's gone now. We just have to face that." He says holding my head against his chest.

"He killed him." I sob into Russell's chest, knowing that Russell had no idea who I was talking about.

"Who killed him, Lorraine?" Russell asks me, demanding to know with his palms clutching my shoulders. Russell had been so uninvolved with the trial because Linda didn't want to burden him with it. She showed up to all the trials and watched as they accused my dad of murder. And they were right. I guess Linda never told him who actually killed his son.

I shake my head and almost collapse which is exactly what I wanted to do right now.

"WHO KILLED HIM?" Russell screams in my face. I shake in fear and stare at Russell.

"My father." I say, before breaking down again.

"The *hell*." Russell whispers before involuntarily, pulling me back into his arms.

"I'm sorry." I shake, sobbing involuntarily.

"It's okay, Lorraine. It's okay." He repeats as I throw my arms around his neck and he holds me. As much trash that I had heard from Cooper, I knew that he still loved his father and that made me able to trust Russell.

"But he's in jail so we don't have to worry anymore. Do you know where Linda is?" I ask him before letting go of him.

"She's at our house, all broken up. I think seeing you would do her some good. She's so upset over the whole thing." He says, handing me his business card, with his address on it.

"Thank you." I say, before hugging Russell and walking out of the bar.

****

When I pull up at his house, I understand why Cooper was so shaken up about not having enough money to go to college. The family had spent it all on the house. By the looks of it, they probably paid off their mortgage too. I ring the doorbell before trying to turn the handle. It is open. I slowly walk into the house, careful about what step I take and what sounds I make. I grab an umbrella next to the side of the door for protection and walk slowly throughout the house. When I reach the kitchen, I hide behind the wall before taking a deep breath and jumping out. No one is there. That's weird. I would think that Linda would be in the kitchen. Maybe she isn't home.

I walk through the house and check all of the rooms, she still wasn't there. I walk into the kitchen and look around. A door is closed off to the side. I walk slowly over to the door and turn the doorknob slowly. After opening the door, I notice that it is a bathroom. I leave the door open and walk slowly towards the curtain of the shower because I notice someone is in there, taking a bath. I open the shower curtain quickly and see Linda, naked and sitting in a pool of blood. The blood is pouring out from her wrists.

"LINDA!" I scream before calling 911.

"911. What's your emergency?" The operator asks. It reminds me of that night. My head gets foggy as I tell the operator to send an ambulance to Linda's address. As I uncontrollably fade out, I see Cooper lying next to me, staring at me.

"*Lorraine.*" He says before I shut my eyes and pass out.

Next thing I knew, I felt the ground moving beneath me.

"Cooper?" I ask before sitting up.

"It's okay, honey. We are from Lakewood Hospital. Can you tell me your name?" A woman asks me, helping me onto a stretcher.

"Lorraine Lowry." I say smiling before I whisper, "Home of the Lions," thinking of Cooper and Lakewood Hospital.

"Okay, sweetie. We are going to get you and your mother to the hospital as soon as we can." She says, thinking Linda is my mother. I don't say anything about her not being my mother because in a way, for the past couple of days, she has been like a mother to me and I am okay with that.

****

CHAPTER 5:

"Lorraine?" My actual mother asks stepping into my hospital room.

"Mom, everything's fine. I just passed out. I don't even know why they gave me a room." I tell my mother so that she doesn't worry more than she is already doing by the look on her face.

"Okay, okay." She says, holding Johnny's shoulder.

"Hey, Johnny!" I say getting up off of the hospital bed and running over to Johnny.

"Hey, Lorraine. What happened?" He asks in his little kid voice that I love so much.

"Nothing at all, buddy. They just wanted to make sure I was okay. It was like a check-up. You know the ones

Mommy and I take you too?" He nods at me.

"Just like that." I scrunch up his cheeks with my fingers as he giggles at my touch.

"How have you been, buddy?" I pick him up and sit him next to me on the hospital bed. My mother steps out of the room due to a phone call as I watch Johnny's face.

"I've been better. I miss Daddy and Mommy happy. And I miss hanging out with you." Johnny says tears welting up in his eyes.

"Tomorrow, I'll pick you up from school and we can go to Adventure World and have all the ice cream in the world." I tickle him a bit.

He giggles before he asks me, "Promise?"

"I promise." I say, laughing at the smile on Johnny's face.

"Are you sharing a room with somebody?" He asks me, getting up and moving over to get a closer look at the person on the other side of the curtain.

"John, don't—" I try to warn him but it's too late.

"Look, Lorraine! It's a woman!" Johnny says, pointing.

"Johnny, it's not nice to—" When I walk on the other side of the curtain, I watch Linda soundly sleep. I look at her monitors and watch her sleep.

"Are you Mrs. Ross's family?" A doctor asks from behind me.

"N—" My brother starts.

"Yes. We are." I say, cutting my brother off. As my brother and the doctor look at me suspiciously, the doctor says, "Mrs. Ross is in critical condition. She seems to be doing better but we don't know how long this is going to last. She may pull through but she may not."

"And how do we know for sure if she pulls through?" I ask her, curiously.

"Right now, Mrs. Ross is in a mild coma. She can wake up anytime she wants. If she wakes up, she still has a chance of not surviving. She lost a lot of blood and her body is trying to make up for it in any way possible. She has a chance of making it through the coma and being perfectly fine. So I would contact all of your family and check if they could be donors for blood." She says clasping her hands together in front of her.

"What is her blood type?" I ask curiously, holding my brother hostage in front of me.

"AB negative. I would contact your family, friends, anyone you can get to donate really." The doctor said, before walking out of the room.

"What the heck was that?" My brother asks me curiously, confused.

"That was helping out a friend." I say to my brother before taking him with me and checking out of the hospital.

"Do you know that lady?" My little brother asks me as he holds my hand, walking out of the hospital.

"Let's just say she took care of me for a little while." I say recalling the days that I spent with her right after Cooper passed away.

"Lorraine?" Linda asks as I lay down on the sidewalk watching the cars roll by. It was closing time so she was locking up for tomorrow.

"He's gone." I whisper before breaking down again just like I had a few hours ago. After telling Linda that Cooper had passed, I collapsed on the side walk and stayed there for hours until Linda came out of the Bar to close it up.

"I know, honey. But you can't do this to yourself." She says lifting me up by my armpits.

"Man, you're heavy." She mutters before I crack a smile and try to help her help me up.

"Make yourself comfortable." She says pulling out a blanket to put over me.

"We don't really have anywhere comfortable to sleep because this isn't a hotel but I bet the corner booth would be really comfortable for the night." She says knowing that I first met Cooper in the corner booth. I sob silently

*as Linda handed me the blanket and put a glass of water
on the table.*

*"It'll all be okay, Lorraine. I promise." She says before
exiting the bar and locking up. The bar is dark and alone,
just like how I feel inside without Cooper in my life.*

****

I dial the first number on my list and wait for
someone to pick up.

"Hello?" A high pitched man says on the other line.

"Hi. My name is Lorraine Lowry, I'm friends with Linda
Ross. I am hoping I could have a few minutes of your time
to talk about donating blood to her."

"Linda? Is she alright?" The man asks, his voice getting
higher.

"She's in a coma and lost a lot of blood. I am calling to see if you or any family members could donate blood to her. Her blood type is rare and without the blood, she will die." I hope that this guy will be the lucky winner.

"Not interested." The man says into the phone before the line goes dead.

"How rude." I say under my breath before I look over at my brother. He stares at me with confusion. I guess Linda's family weren't good role models for her either.

****

After hours of sitting here, typing in numbers, and waiting for a reply, I finally got a man who claims he is willing to donate. He says his name is Nikolaus and that he is a retired police officer. He asks me to meet him in Linda's hospital room precisely at 1 pm. When I arrived at the hospital at 12:55, I enter Linda's room and wait a couple of minutes for the man who called himself Nikolaus. When a middle-aged man walks in the door, I don't know what to think. He looks awfully familiar but I can't put my finger on who he is.

"Nikolaus?" I ask knowing that it is him.

"Nikolaus Nova." He says, putting his hand out.

"Lorraine Lowry but you already know that." I say, knowing I told him my full name over the phone.

"How is she?" He asks, gesturing toward his foster mother.

"She's alright. She's been hanging on, and right now, that's what we need. Finding this blood is going to put me in a coma too." I say though I know I shouldn't have because that was a sick-twisted joke.

"Anyways, do you know what your blood type is?"

"AB positive." He says shrugging his shoulders.

"I don't know if you can donate. I'm going to go ask one of the doctors." I say before exiting the room, trusting Linda's not-biological son to keep her safe while I'm gone.

"Excuse me, Sir." I say calling one of the doctors over.

"If you have AB positive blood type, could you donate to AB negative?" I ask the man who was nice enough to stop and answer my question.

"No, I'm sorry. But as long as the blood is negative, you can donate to a AB negative person." He says making my job a whole lot easier.

"Thank you so much!" I say before entering the medical room where Nikolaus was sitting next to his mother.

"Good news and bad news, Nikolaus." I say before moving closer to Linda's bedside.

"Good news is I found a donor. The bad news is it's not you."

"I'm not able to donate?" He asks, wondering.

"No. But I found someone who can." I say trying to be hopeful.

"Who?" He asks, hoping for someone to help save his mother.

"Me." I smile at him lightly.

"I have a negative blood type. All negatives can donate blood." I say, smiling at him that we found a solution.

"That's great." He says standing up and keeping his palms on his knees out of awkwardness. As we stand there with nothing to say, his phone rings. He quickly picks it out of his back pocket and answers, "Hello?"

"Hey. I'm actually here now." He says looking at the floor and turning away. I couldn't help but eavesdrop on his conversation with the person on the opposite line.

"You're here?" He says staring out the window.

"I told you it was fine and I could handle it. Why do you never listen to me? Alright." He says into the phone.

"Yeah, she's okay. No, she's asleep. Alright. I'll just see you in a little. Alright. Love you, bye." He says quickly into the phone before shutting it off and slipping it into his back pocket.

He turns around to face me as I pretend I wasn't paying any attention to his conversation. He smirks before speaking.

"My sister is very anxious about our foster mom. She had always been the more caring one even though I know you must know about her crime that was committed a while back." He says, not mentioning anything about what happened.

"Uhhh…No I haven't heard about what she did." I say, before pinching my hand in discomfort.

"Well, Linda basically killed our foster brother and his girlfriend because of her husband that adored him and the girlfriend. Linda was completely jealous of how much attention was being shown to the brother by her husband and well, yeah." I have never heard anything that has made me ponder knowing a person so much.

"Well, my sister is right outside because she doesn't listen to me. Do you mind if she comes in as well?" He asks, moving towards the door.

"Not at all." I say before taking a seat next to Linda, waiting to meet Nikolaus's sister. I heard heels and a voice that were rather familiar before the woman appeared in front of Linda.

"Dr. Nova." I say, standing up and brushing off my jeans.

"Lorraine, what are you doing here?" She asks, clutching her purse to her shoulder.

"I'm here for Linda. Her son was my best friend. He's the one who died." I say, watching Dr. Nova with confusion.

"What are you doing here?" I ask her curiously, though I felt as if I already knew the answer.

"Niko is my older brother. I'm here to see my foster mom." She says, looking down at Linda.

"How do you two know each other?" Niko gestures between the two of us.

"She's my psychiatrist." I say, not hesitating to let him know. I didn't care who knew I had a psychiatrist.

"Oh." He says before, moving towards the window and sitting down.

"How is she?" Joanne asks me.

"She's doing good. Actually, I was just going to give blood because my blood type can help her. They say if she doesn't get enough blood, she could never wake up or worse...well, you know." I tell her, making sure that I don't say anything about her dying to upset her.

She nods and all she says is, "Okay." I leave the room after that and find the doctor that came in and told me about Linda's condition.

"Excuse me, doctor?" I tap her on the shoulder.

"Yes?" She turns towards me and stuffs her hand in her pocket.

"I want to donate blood to Linda Ross." I say, before rolling up the sleeve of my plaid button down.

"Okay. Check in with the nurse and give her your information." She says pointing towards a nurse in a light blueish green uniform.

"Thank you." I said moving to talk to the nurse she pointed to.

"Excuse me, Miss. The doctor over there told me to come over here so I could give blood for Linda Ross." I say, curious if I should stay with her or ask another nurse.

"Okay, follow me." She says moving down the hall and into a closed off room.

"I'll be right back." She says before leaving me alone for a couple of minutes. I wait in the room for what feeling like ten minutes before the nurse comes back with the supplies to take blood.

"How much blood do you think she needs?" I ask the nurse curiously.

"She needs about a liter of blood." She says before slipping the needle into my arm.

"Take as much as you can." I say before I watch the blood from my arm go into a plastic bag.

"I am required to only take one pint." She says watching the blood empty into the bag.

"Take three pints then." I say wanting to help Linda as soon as possible.

"I'm not allowed." She says, holding the bag in her hands.

"Just take it, lady. It's free blood." I say, looking at her.

"Alright." She sighs and rolls her eyes, adding another pint to the cord that was connected to the needle. After a while when she is finished, I say, "Thank you."

After she closes the pints and adds a bandage to my arm, I say, "I think I'm going to head back to Linda." My vision blurs.

"Alright. Are you feeling okay?" The nurse asks me knowing that I was feeling the side effects of low blood pressure because she took more than one pint of blood.

"Fine." I say getting up and walking towards Linda's room.

When I get in the room, my head starts to swirl and my vision gets darker.

"How is she?" I ask walking towards Dr. Nova as I enter through the doorway.

"She's the same. Are you okay, Lorraine? You don't look too good." She says grabbing my arm to steady me.

"I'm good. I just donated three pints of blood." I say, putting a hand against my forehead.

"Three pints! You are going to pass out!" Joanne says, throwing her bag on the floor and running to my aid.

"I feel fine." I say as she holds more of my weight than me.

"You don't look fine. Niko, get a doctor." She says, over her shoulder.

"No! I'm seriously fine." I tell Niko as he stops abruptly due to my words.

"Are you sure? You don't look too good, kid." He says as Dr. Nova continues to hold me up. I take my weight and say, "I'm positive." I walk on my own two feet, carrying my own weight, over to Linda who still looks the same as she did when I left. She looks paler though.

"Did a nurse come in and put my blood into Linda?" I ask, curiously.

"No not yet. But she's going to come any second, I suppose." Niko says, moving closer to Dr. Nova and I, who were stationed next to Linda's bedside.

"Good." I say, feeling queasy.

"Do you mind if I sit down?" I say, sitting down abruptly because of my legs giving out.

"Standing up will get the blood to flow down to your legs." Dr. Nova says helping me stand up.

"I'm getting dizzy." I say, standing up as Dr. Nova helps me to my feet. I stand and walk around a bit, trying to get my head right.

"I'm so dizzy." I say, clutching my head.

"Take it easy there, kid." Niko says holding my arm pits as I almost took a fall.

"I'm okay. Thank you." I say, putting my hand on Niko's chest as my eyes close and I pass out.

****

"COOPER!!!!" I scream watching my father stick a knife into my best friend's side.

"It doesn't matter now, he's gone. So just suck it up and move on with your life." He says, taking the knife out and walking towards me.

"GET AWAY FROM ME!" I scream running away from my father and away from Cooper. When I turn around, my father is gone and the alleyway is gone. Instead, there is a familiar bedroom. One that I used to spend most of my time in when I was a kid.

"Ugh, Mom!" Katherine screams walking into her room and shutting the door hard. She slides down the door in pain. Not physical pain but emotional pain. Something I've never seen on Katherine's face before.

"Are you okay, Katherine?" I ask, sitting beside her.

"She can't see you." Someone says from beside me. I turn my head and sitting next to me is Cooper.

"Coop." I say smiling and touching his face.

"Stop being such a girl." He says smirking.

"Would you stop it? I feel like I haven't seen you in forever." I say a tear slipping down my face.

"Look, I don't have much time so you are just going to have to trust me. Can you do that?" He asks me, wiping away the tear that escaped my eye.

"Of course." I say smiling.

"See, after you left Katherine alone, she had everything go downhill for her. The girls she thought were her *friends abandoned her. Her mother and father are going through a divorce and she has to decide where she wants to live. Her brother is joining the army and she doesn't know how to cope with anything. Since you left, her life went spiraling down. And you need to fix it." He says as we watch Katherine cry into her hands against the door.*

"I'm sorry, Lor." She whispers faintly as I touch her shoulder. Though she can't feel a thing, I still feel like I had to do that. And for once, I actually feel that Katherine meant the words she whispered.

"Shall we?" Cooper says, holding out two hands to help me up.

"We shall." I say, taking them.

When I stand up, we aren't in Katherine's room anymore. We are in my house. As I follow Cooper, I see my mother sitting at the dining room table, a bottle of tequila in her hand. Her head is against the table, clearly asleep while the bottle is ready to spill.

"Is she okay?" I ask Cooper, curiously.

"She just received a phone call that her only daughter just slipped into a coma. How would you react?" He says, looking at me.

"What? I-I'm in a coma?" I ask Cooper, backing away from the scene taking place.

"Lorraine, come here. You are fine. I'm making sure of it. I promise. You aren't going to die. He can't let you die yet." Cooper says, holding out his hands.

"Cooper, what is this? Some twisted dream? I don't want to be here anymore. Take me out of here." I say, covering my eyes.

"Open your eyes. You need to see this before we leave. Lorraine, I need to show you this." He says, holding the hand that is covering my eyes. I slowly pull them off as I notice there is another presence in the room. Behind my mother is my brother. He is standing off to the side, clutching the wall, staring at my mother intently.

"Wake up, Mom." I mutter, biting my nails as my mother stays frozen in her spot against the table.

"Wake up for Johnny, Ma." I say before she snorts and her head shoots up off the table.

"Lorraine!" She yells, before getting up and placing the bottle in the cabinet. She doesn't see my brother standing off to the side. She runs up the stairs and off into her room. I watch as Johnny slowly walks over to the bottle in the cabinet that our mother had just put back. He sees a thousand different bottles down there. And one by one, my brother does the appropriate thing I should have

done years ago; he dumps each and every bottle's contents down the sink and into the drain.

"Good job, bud." I say with a pained expression on my face. He is going through too much that I can't even comprehend right now. For God sakes, he's a five-year-old. He doesn't know how to cope with any of this. Especially now that I'm in a coma.

"What do I do, Coop? Tell me what to do." I say crying.

"You know what to do about Johnny. As for your mother, you know where to take her to pull her out of this. You did it once before, do it again." He says talking about a problem that happened a year ago, though I never told Cooper about it. I didn't ask because I knew that he knew because someone wanted him to.

"Mom, what's going on?" I asked my mother who was packing a suitcase in her room, the look of embarrassment running across her face.

She turned around and saw me. I watched as she came over to me and put her hands on my shoulders while saying, "I have to go away for a little while. I'll be back sooner than you know it though." She hugged me while I realized why she's leaving. A pamphlet was lying open on her bed that read, "Atlantic Coast Rehabilitation & HealthCare Center. Ocean County's Premier Nursing Care Center!"

"You're what they call an alcoholic, right?" I asked her with tears clouding my vision. I had heard my father use the term toward my mother once and smart enough, I looked it up.

According to Google, everyone's favorite search engine, alcoholism is defined as, "a chronic disease characterized by uncontrolled drinking and preoccupation with alcohol."

"How wo-would you even know what that-uuhh-is?" She asked me, turning away and throwing the pamphlet into her suitcase.

"Because Dad said it once. You have a drinking problem, don't you?" I watched as her back stiffened and she grew uncomfortable with where this conversation was going. All of a sudden, I laughed. I don't know why but I kept laughing. I laugh until my tears of humor and amusement turn into tears of sadness and disappointment.

"I thought you were supposed to be our mother. Not some booze-drinking junkie who decides to chug a whole bottle of whiskey whenever she feels like it. You are supposed to be the adult because Dad is always away. Instead, I'm the adult when Dad is away. And even when he is here, I'm still the adult." I yelled at her. I was 15. High school was becoming too much and I had to take care of my three-year-old little brother, and I was taking care of my mother, an adult who was old enough to take care of everybody in the world.

"Well then, I don't have to tell you to take care of the house, do I?" She said before picking up her suitcase and walking down the stairs. I listen as the front door slammed shut before I walked into my brother's room.

"It's going to be okay, Jon Jon." I said rubbing his stomach with my finger. He smiles up at me helpless as I think about how he might not grow up with a mother due to her drinking habits.

"Cooper, I don't want to see much more." I say, holding my head.

"Hey, it's okay. We only have a couple more." He pulls my head to look up at him.

"Listen to me, don't mope around about me leaving. I'm happy up here. I want you to meet someone, though." He says bringing my attention to a garden. It is beautiful. Flowers surrounded Cooper and I in a circular

formation. A path formed out of flowers when Cooper steps towards someone in the distance.

"Cooper," I whisper, staring at the flowers that are forming under his feet.

"They are beautiful, aren't they?" He says, seeing my reaction towards them. I nod and follow him, grabbing his hand while watching the flowers form under my feet as well. Before I know it, the woman who was miles away is now within touching distance.

"Lorraine, I would like you to meet, Laura Lovett." Cooper says, still clutching my hand.

"Hi, Ms. Lovett." I say shaking her hand, trying to show a little respect.

"Pleasure to meet you, love. Please call me Laura." She says smiling, her British accent overpowering her words.

I smile at her before looking at Cooper. As I look back at Laura, I notice she is staring at me.

"She's quite beautiful, Coop." She says eyeing me down now.

I chuckle and watch Cooper and Laura make eye contact for more than a second, as if they were sharing a conversation in their heads.

"If I may ask you both, what is the importance of being here right now? I mean, it really is a pleasure meeting you, Ms. Lovett, but I'm not sure what is has to do with this obscene journey Cooper is trying to take me on." I say while keeping my head in order and not being rude at the same time.

"Coop, you didn't tell her who I am?" She says, laughing. I smile at her laugh because it's beautiful in a perfect way.

"I thought she would figure it out." He says, smiling at me while I am getting frustrated.

"Is someone going to let me in on who you are?" I ask glancing back and forth between the two. As I'm watching their faces and the similarities that they seem to have in common, I remember Cooper telling me something a while ago.

"College is coming soon and it looks like if I want to go, I'm going to have to get a scholarship. My dad can barely pay for us to survive now, you know? And my mom, well she left us when I was small." He said looking someplace else.

"I'm sorry."

"It's okay. I barely knew her. It doesn't hurt me as much as it hurts my dad." He shrugs.

"I don't know why I didn't see it before. Mrs. Ross, I'm so sorry." I say holding out my hand for her to shake.

"It's alright, love. He only looked like me when he was little. He is an exact replica of his father now." She says, looking at me while shaking my hand and then looking up at Cooper.

"Hey, not an exact replica." He says, pointing a finger at his mother.

"Not an exact replica." She repeats, before looking back at me.

"How did you get so lucky to have a girl like this one in your life?" She asks Cooper, smiling.

"I don't know. She was looking all beautiful in the corner booth and I sort of just fell." He says, squeezing my hand and smiling down on me. I smile up at him and watch

from the corner of my eye as his mother stares at the both of us as we look at each other. I watch her from the corner of my eye, uncomfortable.

"Mom, you're making me uncomfortable." He says, watching my eye line.

"Sorry, sorry." She says, holding up her hands in surrender.

"I just wanted to see the connection." She says before saying, "Well, Coop is kicking me out so off I'll be. It was a wonderful meeting you, darling." She puts her arms around my back.

"It was wonderful to meet you, too." I say, returning the hug.

"I'll be leaving now." She says, before giving Coop a kiss and disappearing into thin air.

"She is beautiful." I say, staring into the air she just disappeared into.

"She heard you." He says, pointing into the distance. And sure enough, Laura Lovett-Ross is staring at us from the distance, smiling.

"I don't care. She's beautiful." I say, saying it again so I can rub it in to Cooper.

"You're beautiful." He says, pulling me to his chest.

"Thank you. You're not that bad yourself." I say, putting my arms around his neck, knowing something is going to happen.

"Come on. Next place." He says, pulling my hands apart and taking one of them in his own. I felt a pang of

rejection but I knew that we had to get moving. When we took a step, we were transported into a house I had recently been familiar with. I watched as we entered through the walls and walked into the dining room.

"The only person left in this house is—" I watch him by the table, drinking the glass of whiskey. As he jugs the glass, he gets up and throws it against the wall.

"What is he so mad at?" I ask, curiously.

"Me leaving and not having a chance to fix things. Sometimes, you lose the people you love without actually telling them how much you love them. I need you to fix that for me." He says, pointing towards his father.

"What do you want me to say to him?"

"Tell him I love him and that I know he loves me. Tell him I forgive him. And if he ever wants to talk to me, tell him to talk to you."

"Why me?" I ask, pointing a finger at myself.

"Because you knew more about me than anybody on that planet. And I think if he asks you a question, you could answer it as if it was me. Plus, for the last couple of days of my life, you held my heart. If he wants to talk to me, he can talk to my heart." He says, smiling at me.

I smile back because for the first time, I see Cooper. Not the Cooper who was mauled against the dumpster. Not the Cooper who was dead and staring at me like in my nightmares. Not the Cooper who was wounded and spitting up blood on me. The real Cooper, the one who was standing next to me right now. He may not actually be real though.

"Okay." I say, before we get transported into different scenery. This time, instead of his house, we are at the prison.

"I can't do anything with my father. I'm sorry but that is something I can't do. He ruined his chance such a long time ago by not even being there. Plus, he murdered you. I hate him for what he—"

"Lorraine, he murdered me, not you. Calm down for a second. I just want you to tell your father that I forgive him and that I knew it was him when he killed me. I've always known about Linda's story. I researched her for crying out loud. I knew his new family, which was you, and when you walked into the bar, I recognized you from the moment I saw you. I just had no idea he was trying to get revenge when he pulled me into the alleyway." Cooper tells me, making my head spin even though I don't even know where my head was at right now.

"Cooper," I whisper, watching his face as he didn't know what was coming.

"What the hell are you talking about?" I scream watching his face.

"You can't just say that! What? Did you plan this? You just-you can't say stuff like that! It was a mistake and you had no idea! You don't know what you are talking about, okay? When you saw me, you didn't know me." I say, shaking my head, outraged.

"Lorraine, I knew your name before you knew mine. You need to face this." He says, holding my hands that are covering my eyes.

"Why are you doing this to me? Why are you telling me this now? For forgiveness, for pity?" I ask, my heart hurting.

"Lorraine, I want you to know—"

"Just stop this! I don't want to do this anymore." I say, covering my ears.

"Lorraine, would you just listen to me?" He yells and grabs my hands, slowly peeling them off my ears.

"Look, when you walked into the bar, I wanted to hate you. But when I saw you get frustrated, that hate went away and love came into my heart. Alright, Lorraine? That's it. As for your father, I didn't know he wanted revenge. Calm down and breathe." He says, bending down and staring into my eyes.

"Why do you do this? Why do you always act like the good guy even when bad things happen to you?" I ask him, trying to understand why he was being so graceful about things.

"It's over. It happened. Get stronger. Move on. Though I can't move on because I'm dead." He says, laughing. "That's not funny." I say, watching as he actually laughed at that.

"Sorry, I'm trying to lighten the mood. After all, we are by your father's prison cell." He says, smiling. I smile back at him and turn my head to watch my father lay on the steel bed that they gave him. I watched the man who killed my best friend suffer silence for pretty much the rest of his life. Unless, if down the line the judge decides to give him parole.

"So that's all I have to do here?" I ask him, making sure that's all.

"Tell him I forgive him and that I knew it was him. That's it. Last place." He says, watching my face as we arrived in a cemetery.

"What are we doing here?" I ask him worrying. His face shifts into deep solemn.

"Cooper?" I ask calling his name. He moves into a certain position as if a wall is blocking him from passing and he points to a headstone in the distance. I follow the finger and walk slowly towards the headstone. I turn back and Cooper is watching me with pain-filled eyes. Taking a deep breath, I move closer towards the headstone. When I reach it, I keep looking up until the anxiousness is eating me up. The headstone reads,

"HERE LIES

LINDA ALLISON ROSS

BELOVED MOTHER, FRIEND, WIFE, AND SISTER."

My eyes cloud and so does my judgement.

"No." I whimper watching the headstone get foggy due to my tears.

"NO!" I scream holding the 'o.' I turn and see Cooper staring at me with tears running down his face for me. "WHY?" I scream, not focusing on the tears running down my face right now. I run to Cooper, walking through headstones. Cooper catches me and holds me in his arms.

"I'm sorry." He whispers into my ear.

"Me too." I say, crying into Cooper's white t-shirt. This isn't real. None of this is, I don't want it to be.

"It's real, Lorraine." Cooper says, answering the questions floating around in my head.

"What is?" I ask, sniffling and wiping my nose as he lets me down.

"All of it." He explains.

"Including this?" I ask, unsure if this could be the reality for Linda.

"This is the reality." He says, frowning. The curves of his face go down in sadness and his once excited and pleased face is now hurt.

"What happens now?" I ask him, still not accepting the reality that Linda will be gone when I get back.

"We say our goodbyes." He says, looking up.

"No. I can't say goodbye now, I mean I just found out—" And then in this reality or this dimension or wherever we are, Cooper Allen Ross crashes his lips against mine. It is a miracle and a blessing and everything that I wished it could've actually been while he was alive. When Cooper pulls away, he stares at me. I could feel his eyes staring at my closed ones, my lips still in kissing position.

"I've been waiting for that forever." I say, opening my eyes and seeing a whole different Cooper.

"I know. But we've only known each other for less than a week, you shouldn't have gotten your hopes up." He says, laughing.

"Just kiss me." I say, pulling his neck down to mine to lock our lips together. It felt like forever until Cooper pulls away and says, *"I have to go now."*

"I don't want you to." I say, wanting him to say with me forever.

"You still have unfinished business down there, Lorraine. You aren't allowed to stay here." He says, watching my eyes as they filled with loneliness once again.

"I miss you down there." I say, not even knowing where I was going right now on the Compass Rose.

"I miss you up here. Keep your options open, Lorraine. Who knows? People might come back into your life." He says, kissing me one more time quickly.

"You know I'm in love with you, right?" He says, releasing his hold on me.

"I'm in love with you, too." I say, kissing his cheek.

"It's time to go. I love you." He says, before I close my eyes and open them a minute later.

****

"Lorraine?" Dr. Nova asks me, watching my eyes slowly open.

"Dr. Nova, what are you doing here?" I ask, searching around for some sign of Cooper. The drawing. Where did I put the drawing?

"No." I say, not paying attention to whatever the heck Dr. Nova is going to say. Where is my drawing? I turn my head to look next to where I am laying down and there it is. The drawing. It is standing up against some vase with no flowers with the note sitting on the table. I let out a deep breath and smile. Looking up, I think of my conversations with Cooper. Maybe they were all in my head but they were good conversations.

"Dr. Nova, I—" And then I look at her. She has bags under her eyes, she has bloodshot eyes, and she looks like she has been crying for hours.

"Are you alright? What's going on?" I ask, getting up out of the bed.

"It's alright, just lay back down. The doctors will be in shortly." She says, waiting with me.

"Dr. Nova, is Linda alright?" I ask, watching her facial expressions take a turn for the worst when I mention Linda.

"She died, didn't she?" I ask her, tears flooding up in my eyes. She nods and I break down crying. All the realities that Cooper showed me are true. They happened. Now I have to fix some of them. But for the time being, I mourn over Linda Allison Ross, a beloved mother, sister, wife, and friend, whom, just like Cooper, I could not save.

****

I don't know what today is or what time it even is. All I know is that I am getting released and I'm going home to see my mom, my brother, fix things for Cooper with my father, and with Russell. When I leave the hospital in the front seat of Dr. Nova's car, I think back to when I was sitting on the couch, watching re-runs of "I Love Lucy." I never thought any of this would happen to me. I was lonely and heartbroken then. Now, I'm the same but I've become a different person. A person who actually deserves to be happy. Lucas James Kelly never deserved my love and he was never going to get it again, not even a glimpse. Or so I thought.

****

"This is me." I say, pointing toward my house. It is a small, decent sized house with a big porch in the front that I used to sit on when I was little.

The house is like a cottage compared to Cooper's house. It is made up of different shades of orange and red bricks, unlike all of the houses on the block, which were a bunch of cookie-cutters and shingles. My house has a small roof that came down to the front and ran across the back. It has a small window that is located in the closet, shaped like a stop sign. The door is located on the left while big covered windows are located on the right. They open the house while the brick made the house seem caved in. On the side of the house is another door located inside the driveway, which has a nice old gate that I used to love showing my mom I could open when I was a kid.

Our Honda isn't parked inside the driveway, which makes me nervous but I'm sure it is in our handmade garage that my father and I worked on together for a large amount of days. From day to night we stayed out there and made the garage. We used to be close but then, besides the murder, he got a job promotion and he started to work more often. I grew up and he got a bigger role in his company, making his time with his family even more sparse.

"Do you want me to walk you to the door?" Dr. Nova asks me, curiously just wanting to make sure I am okay.

"I'm fine but thank you." I say smiling, trying to open the door.

"Here, let me." Joanne says as she unlocks the door on her side before reaching over and clasping the handle back, opening the door.

"Thank you." I smile. I look up at her before getting out of the car and shutting the door lightly.

"Wait, Lorraine!" She says, getting out of the car and following me as I open the gate. She runs up to me, leaving her car to idle. I shut my eyes tight before opening them and watching her run up to me, holding out my bag that I had forgot in the car.

"You forgot this." She says, holding out my bag for me to take. Cooper's drawing is lodged inside my bag, poking out of it.

"Thank you." I smile.

"No problem," She says walking slowly back to the car—"Oh, Lorraine." My head turns quickly as if I was a child and I just heard someone cuss.

"Someone left a message for you in your bag." She says, pointing to the bag. Not at all what I expected.

"Thanks." I say, before reaching out in my bag and searching for a paper with my hands and eyes.

"You got it." She says before watching me a second. When I find the note, she gets in the car. I slowly take my time and read what is in neat handwriting on the little piece of paper Dr. Nova told me about.

If I would have known we were related, I would have said something. But I only found out from when the doctor brought in your medical records. If you can, meet me with my brother at Billy's, which I'm sure you are familiar with, at around 5. Bring your little brother. I would like to meet him if that's okay with you.
Joanne Nova.

It ends there. I don't know if I should go but I want to badly. Not only is she the only way I can find out the truth but she is the last hope I have of a family; family sticks together.

****

CHAPTER 6:

Time is ticking by and five o'clock is just around the corner. I had just taken a shower, pulled up my long but short hair very nicely, and I had applied little to no makeup to my eyes and face. I placed a blush red lipstick to my lips, bringing out the color of my eyes with a little bit of makeup. When I thought I was finished, I knocked on my brother's door, careful to not upset him.

"Johnny?" I call out, making sure he is still alive in there. I have wanted to talk to him all day but I haven't gotten the chance yet.

"Johnny?" I call out again. Instead of calling out another time, I just slowly open the door, careful not to open too fast because I didn't want to scare him.

"Hello?" I say with a smile on my face. I watch the window across the room from me, open while the curtain is flowing outside it. Johnny is gone.

"Johnny!" I yell, scared that I lost the only thing besides Cooper that truly matters to me.

"No, no, no!" I yell, looking down the window. It is a pretty far fall because the steps to the outside door of the basement were outside Johnny's window. The fall could have instantly killed him.

"Johnny!" I scream, wanting more than anything for my brother to come up behind me and scare me. Scare me a million times just so that I wouldn't have to face being without him.

"Johnny." I say, tears filling up in my eyes. I put my hands on my forehead and balanced my elbows outside the window. Arms wrap around my leg causing it to release its tenseness and causing my head to turn around. His arms are now around my waist, his small head in my lap, and his small feet just inches away from mine.

"Johnny." I say, before bending down and hugging him tightly.

"Lorraine, not so tight." He says as if being choked.

"Alright, bud." I say hugging him lighter now with air between us.

"You look pretty, Lorraine." He says smiling, letting go of his arms that were once around me.

"You do too, bud." I say, ruffing up his hair.

"Hey!" He says, before fixing his hair in the mirror.

"Come on, bud. I want to talk to you." I say, taking his hand and yanking his arm into my room. I throw him on the bed, giggling, before he sits up straight and waits for our conversation to begin.

"How old is daddy, bud?" I ask him, trying to figure out how old he even is.

"57?" He asks me, shrugging his shoulders.

"I don't even know, myself, but somewhat around there. See before Daddy met Mommy, he had another wife. Her name was Linda. Linda and Daddy wanted babies so they adopted three kids. Now they are all grown up but Linda and Daddy split after Linda did some bad things. Mommy and Daddy got married after that and had us. After that, Daddy did some bad things to Linda. They were unforgivable." I say, shaking my head.

"Do you understand what I am trying to say?" I ask him, knowing I was lost at my first words.

"So basically, Daddy had another wife and had three kids. Linda did bad things and they broke up. Mommy and Daddy had us and then Daddy did bad things. Is that all?" He asks me, crossing his arms, acting like a know-it-all.

"Basically, something bad happened and one of them went away because of it. Now there are only two kids left." I say, trying to get myself to understand this as well.

"Did one of them get killed with a knife?" He says, curiously.

"How would you know that, bud?" I ask him, sitting on the bed with him this time, instead of crouching on the floor.

"I was watching the news with Mom. She was crying but I was watching it closely and a guy died because he was stabbed with a knife by Daddy." Johnny said it, without looking the least bothered by it.

"That's the bad thing Daddy did that I was telling you about." I say, watching Johnny stare at me. I was struggling to hold back from thinking of Cooper and in that cemetery, how our lips clung to each other. How we couldn't let each other go.

"You knew the guy that was killed, didn't you?" Johnny asks me, putting points together that I was never able to do at five-years-old.

"How do you figure this stuff out?" I ask. He shrugs and smiles.

"Well, I did know him and he didn't deserve to die." I say, shaking my head.

"So, why did you want to tell me all this?" He asks, banging his legs against the bottom of my bed.

"Because the children that are sort of our siblings asked

me to meet them at this place. They asked me to bring you too. So I wanted to know if you wanted to come." I ask, hoping I don't get a five-year-old tantrum.

"Sure." He says, shrugging. "As long as I get to fix my hair and wear my good shoes." He smiles at me.

"Of course, bud. Go all out." I say, ruffing his hair again before he runs off to get ready. I laugh and get ready myself before we go out to actually sit down and have a meal with our siblings that I never knew we had.

****

"Come on, bud." I say, getting out of the car and unbuckling Johnny from his seat.

"Let's go." I say, walking up to Billy's Bar. The closed sign is placed on the door, sad looking now that Linda wasn't in there even when it was closed. I walk in, hearing the sad doorbell ring.

"Go away, we're closed!" Someone says from the back. I notice the voice instantly and follow where it came from. I keep Johnny behind me, noticing that he follows me wherever I go, probably because he is scared. I peek in the door I heard the noise come from and see Russell hunched over the inventory, drinking away his sorrows.

"Oh, Russ." I say before letting go of Johnny's hand and watching as Russ, looks at me and then looks at Johnny. His eyes welt up with tears and his face turns a blush red.

"What's your name, son?" Russ asks, wanting to know more about the little boy standing in his doorway. I am leaning next to Russ, noticing this. Johnny looks at me before saying, "Johnny, Sir."

"Johnny boy." Russell says, letting it roll off his tongue.

"It's a pleasure, Sir." Johnny says, holding out his hand and walking closer to Russell. Russ turns to me and smiles before he takes Johnny's hand in his and shakes it.

"Nice handshake you got there, John." Russell says, getting himself up to avoid the child seeing him drunk.

"Thank you, Sir. I've been practicing with my mother." He says, holding his head high.

"Johnny, can you go in the hallway for a second? If there is any trouble, you just scream, got it?" I ask him, watching him turn his back before saying,

"Yes, ma'am." He leaves Russ and I alone to talk. Russ collapses on the ground while I attempted to catch him but it fails.

"Russ, you need to stop this. My mother is like this. And I don't want to see you turn into her. Please." I say, letting his arm rest against the wine coolers and sitting down beside him.

"I have nobody left. I had Cooper, he's gone. I had Linda, she's gone. Nobody left to love me and nobody for me to love left." He says, taking another swig of the alcohol in his hand.

"Would you stop this? You have me, okay? I'll love you and you'll love me. I promise. Cooper—he wanted me to tell you that he loves you and that he knows you love him, okay? He knows. So stop blaming yourself for your mistakes because he forgives you and he loves you, Russ. And he's with Laura right now. He's okay." I say, holding Russ's hand. He breaks down sobbing. I pull him into a hug.

"I can't believe he's gone." He sobs.

"I know. But the best thing to do right now, is to accept it and move on. That's exactly what Cooper wants me to do. And I expect the same from you, Russ." I say, because Cooper wants me to fix things. So that's just what I am going to do. One down, four to go.

****

I leave Russ alone to clean things up, knowing that instead he would probably pass out. I turn the sign into open and watch as the people start pilling in. I call my brother out to help me but even with his help, it is too little. I know what I have to do. I dial her number and listen to the ringing of the phone. I wait for her to pick up and when she finally did, I said, "Katherine, come down to Billy's bar. I need your help." I say before ending the phone call and calling the next person that I need help from.

"Mom, I need your help. I need you to come to *Billy's Bar*. I'll explain everything here, just come." I say, before ending the phone call just like I did Katherine. I popped out my vocal cords and announced, "Hey guys, I'm sorry that we haven't been in service for a couple of days. I'm waiting for two people to arrive so if you could just be patient with me, I'll explain everything when they get here."

****

My mother and Katherine walk in at the exact same time, making my life a hell of a lot easier.

"Take a seat." I say, watching my mother and my ex-best friend, who I am going to mend things with, sit down at the corner booth; the one that had meant the most to me out of all the seats in the bar.

"Okay, welcome to *Billy's Bar,* everybody. My name is Lorraine and I'm sorry that we haven't opened in a while but I should let you know about some things before you order. When I arrived here for the first time ever, I thought it was some crappy diner started by a woman with a lot of money. When I sat down at that corner booth, right there," I say, pointing to where my mother and Katherine were sitting right now, "A man came up to me and asked if I was alright. He didn't know my name, he didn't know my story, and he didn't know what the hell was going on inside my head. He just saw I was upset. That was an act of kindness by Cooper Allen Ross.

"I later got to know Cooper and we became friends in less than a week. But in less than a week, a man hit me in the head with a knife, tied me to a chair, and tried to kill me.

"Cooper Allen Ross, the stranger I met at that corner booth while he was working here, saved my life. Sadly, I can't say I returned the favor. Cooper died that night protecting me from my own father. Though a vicious crime, my father committed it because his ex-wife, Linda, the owner of this bar, killed his favorite son and his girlfriend. My family is far, far from normal and I promise you that I am far from perfect. This bar is far from perfect. We have no workers. Cooper and Linda are gone.

"We have a big story to tell though. And it's actually quite shocking and interesting. Our backstory could go on forever. I could sit here and just blab on about my life and how this started with me and one simple, now meaningless, little heartbreak that I thought was the end of the world. Billy's Bar is where my story started and I hope now that you know about some of the things that went on here, you will want to be a better person. Cooper had no idea he was going to die and save someone's life that day. He had no idea how much time he had left.

"Make the most out of your life and don't settle for anything that isn't as great as you want it to be. Cooper taught me that even though family can be cruel, hurtful and can take a step away from your life, that they are always family and you will always love them and they will always love you. Be grateful for the people sitting next to you. Don't take them for granted like I did Cooper. We will be serving now. Thank you for your time." I say, before glancing over at my mother and Katherine, who were beginning to tear up, and glancing over at my brother, who was smiling uncontrollably. Then, I peeked over at Joanne and Niko, who were sitting at the next table over from the corner booth, both looking directly at me and smiling. I even got a wink from Dr. Nova. Claps rounded the room, making me smile proudly for the unprepared little monologue I just said in front of a crowd full of people.

"In less than a week, so much can happen, right?" Russell says from behind me, a smile planted on his face.

"Ready to go to work?" I say, before handing him a rag.

"More than you know." He says, before we both got to work waiting tables. When my Mom and Katherine join us, grabbing hats, aprons, and rags, I am so thrilled that I lift my head up and smile at the sky. I can feel Cooper being proud of me right now. I didn't fix all of the problems between my mother, Katherine, and my brother, but at least for now, they are happy. And that's all I could hope for.

****

"Order for Table 6." I say, watching as my brother holds the plates sturdy in his hands and brings them over, without dropping them. I walk with him towards the table, plates in my hands as well.

"Thank you." The woman says, smiling at my brother. When he leaves, she looks up at me and says, "You are really brave. You know that, Lorraine?"

"Thank you." I say, as she clutches onto my hand. I feel like I can really inspire people with my story and how I didn't suffer from depression or turn to alcohol and drugs. I just kept moving forward even after Cooper and Linda died, my father killed them and went to jail, my mother turned to alcohol, my brother struggled with loneliness, and my ex-best friend was suffering through what had to be the hardest stages of someone's lives. Moving forward is the secret.

I walk away and leave the couple to eat their food. It's about eight o'clock in the evening and it's been three hours exactly since I walked through the bar doors.

"Lorraine, go take a break." Russell says, knowing that I had yet to sit down with my siblings, who arrived late but were happy to stay while I helped around the Bar. My brother had introduced himself, took their orders, and had been their waiter the whole night. Now, he is sitting down at their table and playing around with Niko while Joanne is watching the boys get along perfectly. I wipe my hands on my apron, smile at Russell while thanking him with my eyes and walking over to the table where my family was sitting.

"Hi, guys." I say, sitting down across from Joanne.

"Hey, Lorrie."

"Hi," I say smiling.

"What did I miss?"

"Johnny and Niko are playing napkin football." She says, laughing as Niko flicks the napkin shaped like a triangle into the goal that Johnny made with his fingers.

"Aw, are you kidding? You get one every time!" Johnny says, picking up the napkin football and throwing it at Niko. He sits there and laughs before picking my brother up and moving over by the bar to order drinks or something. I turn around and watch them leave.

"You know, I really liked what you said before." She says, smiling at me. I turn my head and watch her, "What I said about what?"

"About family and about being perfect and pretty much everything. It was just a speech that should have been written down." She says, smiling at me.

"Thank you." I laugh, "You know I didn't really prepare any of this."

"I know. It's fun watching my sister scramble for words." She says, hitting my shoulder playfully.

"Your sister?" I smirk.

"Well, that's what we are, aren't we? We're sisters." She says, breaking out into a huge smile.

"I like the sound of that. And by the way, I was totally not scrambling for words." I get up, following the boys to the bar.

"You were. You were staring around like 'What the hell do I say next?'" She laughs and links arms with me as we walk over to the boys at the bar.

"Don't get drunk on me, Niko. I need you to drive home." Joanne says, smiling. Her smile is the brightest I've ever seen. Even on the day I met her it wasn't this bright. Maybe it is the moment but maybe she is just genuinely happy right now. And that made me happy. Her best friend died and so did mine, so she became mine and I became hers.

"Okay, okay." Niko says, holding his hands up in surrender as he sips his beer that he ordered from the bar. He glances over at me.

"So what do I call you now? He wants to be called big shot." Niko says, pointing to my brother.

"You can call me, sister." I say, winking at him. He laughs and glances at his own sister. He watches her smile before saying, "Okay, sister."

I laugh as the long and beautiful conversations with my family begin. We were just missing one person: Niko and Joanne's brother. But I knew he was with us in the chair beside Niko. For Cooper was once there, and he always will be. Maybe just like Cooper, Anderson will be here, watching over all of us. Like the very special angel he is.

****

Sometimes in our lives, we don't know what to say or when to say it. This is one of those moments. I have no idea what to say to make my mother better. No words, no feelings, just nothing. Time is ticking and I don't know if I actually want to follow what Cooper said. Fix things with my mother? Make her feel better? What about me? Who is supposed to fix me? It is around 9. An hour ago, I was laughing and smiling with the people I want to watch me grow up. I walk through the front door of my petite house and take off my shoes in the front. Still clutching onto my hand, Johnny does the same.

"Hey, Jon Jon?" I ask, tugging on his hand. His eyes are slowly closing, tired from the long day of not being lonely.

"Mhm?" He hums, barely looking at me.

"Thank you." I say, before picking him up and moving towards his bedroom.

"Mhm." He hums again, putting his head in the crook of my neck.

"Good night," I say, all smiley while climbing our stairs.

"Good night," He shuts his eyelids over his beautiful light crystal blue eyes, similar to mine. His breathing became steady as he clutches onto my hand. He falls asleep in my arms like he did when he was a baby.

****

I sit down in my office chair, turning on my Mac in front of me. Now that my dad is no longer supplying the green, my mom is going to have to step it up. I search the internet quick for any jobs that qualify my mother but to my luck, there are none. I figure I would talk to Russell tomorrow and see if he could get me and my mother a job at Billy's.

After tirelessly searching for a job that isn't even for me, I open a fresh document in Word and start typing. I don't really know what I am typing but I know I want to write something really great. Something that people can cry about, call their friends and gossip about after they finish reading it, smile about when they come to a good scene, and scream about how good the ending is when they finish it.

So I started typing. I didn't realize what time it was until I finished the prologue and up to chapter five. I didn't know what would happen next, I didn't know what would become of the writing, and I didn't know what I would think of it in the end. But I knew that the feeling of knowing the next sentence to write right away, the feeling that comes with your fingers pressed against the keys of the computer, the feeling that your body gives off when your fingers are moving faster than your brain. It's electric and that's why I love writing random things that form a page, that form a story that someone is going to pick up, sit down and read. It's unique, special, and nobody else has those same exact words in their heads or in their books. Writing is unique and different. And I like this different.

I go to sleep at five o'clock in the morning with the feeling of greatness spreading through my body and sixty-three pages of a book finished.

****

The morning or at least when I wake up, I feel compelled to open the computer and starting to type again. Instead, I walk toward the door and turn my head; nobody in the hallway. I walk down stairs and take the flour out of the cabinet and all the supplies to make pancakes from scratch. I mix the batter that I made before pouring it perfectly in the pan. I may not know how to crack open a beer but I do know how to make a mean batch of pancakes.

Putting my first set of four pancakes on a plate, I carry it up with a glass of orange juice to my mother's room, trying to put across a nice gesture. After all, I am going to have to have a conversation with her about her drinking. It is getting obsessive again. I walk up the stairs and turn the corner to walk into her room. Watching her sleep, I put the plate and the drink on the side of her counter.

"Mom," I say, shaking her awake. She jolts up with a start and sits up quickly.

"What?" She says, softly her voice heavy and dark. And then I see it. There are several bottles of alcohol next to her side, one of them within her grasp.

"Get up, eat your food, and get dressed. We are going somewhere." I say, pulling her suitcase out from under the bed.

"Where are we going?" She asks like a child.

"Somewhere where you'll be happy." I pack away clothes for her. I throw them in the bag with rage. She is doing it again but this time, I would do something about it.

"Get up." I say, before lugging the suitcase downstairs as she watches me with curiosity. Dropping the suitcase at the front door, I pull out my phone and search for the number online. When I dial it, I don't give it a second of thought. I know my mother needs this.

Cooper said, *"... talk to her. And pull her out of this. You did it once before, do it again."* And that's exactly what I was going to do.

"Atlantic Coast Rehabilitation & HealthCare Center. Ocean County's Premier Nursing Care Center, my name is Lana. How can I help you?" Lana asks on the other side of the phone sounding ecstatic that I called.

"Hi. My mother has a drinking problem. What can you do?" I say, not knowing really where to start.

"If you drop her off, we can take her until we think she is better. We have doctors here that can help her. Will you be dropping her off shortly?" Lana asks me.

"Very shortly. Should I bring anything with her?"

"Clothes and everything she needs to stay for a while. Anything else she needs for a vacation away from home.

Maybe you should bring her license and I think we will handle the rest." Lana says as I could hear the smile in her voice.

"Thank you. Oh, by the way, how should I pay?" I say, rubbing my head.

"We don't worry about the money until she's out of the center. We want to make sure that she is okay and we could help her."

"Should I know about anything else?" I ask, before watching my mother walk down the stairs.

"I think we covered everything. There are different plans if you cannot afford the treatment right now. We have a beautiful facility and a wonderful staff to make her stay even more welcome."

"Thank you." I say, before she ends the phone call and I run upstairs to grab Johnny. I carry him down the stairs and place him in the backseat before throwing my mother's suitcase in the back of the car.

"Get in the car, Mom." I say, before getting in the driver's seat and waiting for my mother to get in the car.

"Not before you tell me where we are going." She puts her hand on her hip.

"Get in the car, Mother." I forcefully say this time.

"Tell me where we are going." She says, acting like Johnny.

"Mom, I really don't need this right now. Get in the car, Billie Holiday." I say, waiting for her to get in.

"Thank you." She says, getting in the car, thinking the name I gave her was a flattering remark. Little does she know, Billie Holiday died of alcoholism and I am saving my mother from dying of it too. I lock the doors and drive off quickly saying, "It wasn't a compliment."

****

When I pull up to the center, my mother turns her head and stares out the window.

"This is what you need, Mom. I'm trying to save you from yourself. Let me help you." I say, hoping that she isn't mad and that she knows she needs this. But she didn't say a word. She just unlocks the doors, opens the trunk, says goodbye to Johnny, and leaves.

"Hey, Mom." I call out as she is walking towards the center. She turns around, startled that I call for her.

"I love you." I say, smiling at her for doing this. This would help our family. I could get a job right now and support the family if my mother can't. She smiles back and runs at me with her arms open, leaving her suitcase behind.

"I love you so much. Thank you." She says, clutching my body in her arms.

"I love you too, Ma. Just get better and we'll be here waiting for you when you come out. I promise." I say, kissing her cheek.

And then she says something I never thought she would say, "I'm sorry."

It takes me by surprise. I don't realize it but it's just like when Christmas time rolls around and you are anxious to get the presents that you know are waiting for you to open under your tree. That was the feeling that I had felt all those times I've been waiting for my mother to say "I'm sorry" but I was never given the chance to go downstairs and open those presents. Now I had that chance for the first time in forever. And it is wonderful to finally get the chance to scream, "I got a present!" or "I've been waiting for this for so long!"

"Thank you." I sigh in relief. It is finished. "I'm sorry" couldn't fix a lot, but it was a start to fixing most of the problems between my mother and me. I can believe in hope when there is a start; hope for things to get better when she gets better. If she has to go away to get better, then so be it. But my mother was going to get better, with this center's help or not. I am not going to let her wake up to being surrounded by bottles of alcohol ever again.

****

I take Johnny out for the day, wanting him to experience what it is like to not be lonely. I don't really plan anything special but I know that whatever I can fit in would be good for Johnny. As long as he is moving around and has a smile on his face, I would be happy too.

"Where do you want to go, bud?" I ask him as he stares out the window in the middle of the backseat. He shrugs his shoulders.

"Anywhere that you've never been before that you want to go?" I ask him, curiously as I cruise around the block from our house. He shrugs his shoulders again.

"Close your eyes." I order as he slowly closes his eyes.

"Imagine your idea of a perfect day. Where would you go? Who would it be with? What would you see?" I say, as I watch his eyeballs dance around under his eyelids in the mirror. I park on the side of the road, next to our house.

"Now open your eyes. Do you know what your perfect day is?" I ask him, watching his eyes slowly open and a smile slowly appear.

"I want to go see Daddy!" He says, shouting at me. My face goes red with embarrassment.

"Johnny, we can't go see Daddy. Is there anything else?" I ask him, rubbing my forehead while my elbow rests against the steering wheel.

"Yes, but I want to go see Daddy and make sure he's okay. And then we can leave. I promise, only for a little." Johnny says, holding his hands tightly together like the clean-cut five-year-old he is.

"As soon as I say we are leaving, we are leaving. Understand?" I tell Johnny just making sure that I don't regret this. But I know I will as I drive away towards the prison where my dad is being held.

****

 "I want to see Daddy." Johnny says again, pulling on my hand.

"I know, Johnny. He's right in this room." I say, pointing ahead of the security guard, who is leading us into the room where my father told me that he killed Cooper.

"He's right there." I point to my father, who is sitting in a chair, watching us in the plastic in front of him. The orange jumpsuit starts to look normal on him and a beard starts to be a normal look for him as well.

"Daddy!" Johnny runs towards my father, who is blocked by a sheet of plastic in front. John puts his hands up to the plastic, sitting down on the seat in front of our father. My father points me towards the telephone so that we can talk. I pick it up and wait for the sarcastic comments to be said.

"I thought you never wanted to see me again." He smirks.

"Don't get your panties in a twist." I say laughing, "I came because John wanted to see you."

"Is that so? Put him on the phone." He says, glancing down at the kid.

"You better not say anything that you wouldn't want to say to my face or say anything that isn't appropriate for a five-year-old to hear." I say, threatening him.

"I'm still his father you know. I'm not that heartless." Our father smirks.

"You are funny. I can still read lips, you know." I say, before handing the phone to Johnny and waiting for their conversation to be over. I watch my father just in case he pulls something wacko just like he did to get in here.

I wasn't paying close attention because I was focusing on what I was supposed to say to him for Cooper. He had wanted me to say something to my father for him that I forgot about because I had focused on fixing things with the people I actually cared about. So far, I had fixed things with Russell, solved the problem with my mother, and started trying to write. Now I just have to fix things with Katherine, solve things with Lucas even though I know he isn't worth it, talk to my father, and have fun with Johnny..

"Here," Johnny says, stepping down from the chair to let me sit. He stands next to the chair, holding onto the table.

"Speak or forever hold your peace." My father says, speaking into the telephone.

"I slipped into a coma a little while ago. And Linda died." I wait, before speaking out of respect for Linda. "Cooper wants me to say to you that he forgives you for what you did to him. Even though I think it's unforgivable and inexcusable."

"Well, I'm sorry for your loss or whatever but how the hell did Cooper even tell you this?" My father laughs as if I'm the insane one.

"When I was in a coma, I saw him. I don't even think I believe it myself but I saw him and what he showed me actually happened. So I guess I'm stuck believing it." I say, rubbing my forehead once again because I am not sure what to believe.

"I met Joanne and Niko. They are so nice even though they were raised by you." I say, making it hurt. I want him to hurt. Because I've been through more hurt than he'll ever know because of him.

"Johnny has to go to the bathroom but he doesn't want to rush you so when you leave, remember that." My father stares down at the table, changing the subject so easily.

"Okay." I knew he was lying to me, anyways.

"Oh and before I leave, Cooper wants to tell you that he knew it was you. He knew you were my father and he sacrificed himself to save me, anyways. Coward." I spit, before slamming the phone down and walking out of the prison with Johnny by my side and his hand in mine.

When we got into the car, I curiously ask Johnny, "Hey Jon Jon, do you have to go to the bathroom?"

He nods his head and holds his genitals. I realized, my father was telling the truth. I take Johnny out and let him pee in the bushes outside of the road. After that, we drive away from the prison, from my father.

****

"Where to, bud? This is your day for no loneliness, whatsoever." I say, smiling in the rearview mirror.

"I want to work again at Billy's." He smiles.

"You like working there?" I ask him, curiously.

"Mhm." He hums, smiling back at me and listening to the radio.

"Alright. We are off to Billy's." I say, before driving off towards Billy's.

****

When we arrive at Billy's, I notice Russell inside. He is working diligently on something that I can't see through the front window. When I walk into the bar, the bell goes off and Russell jumps. I laugh and Johnny joins in while Russell looks up quickly and sees us. He laughs as well, cleaning up his work.

"What's that?" I ask him, moving with Johnny closer to what he was working on.

"Nothing. Just something for my job." He says, folding his documents up and holding them in his hand.

"To what do I owe the honor?" Russ asks, bowing down to us. Johnny giggles a bit as I smile up at Russ.

"We want to work." Johnny says to Russ.

"Do you, buddy? Well go on and do me a favor, turn that sign to open." Russ says, pointing towards the door. Johnny runs along and turns the sign to open. I laugh and look at Russell. I can't tell if he's happy or not because we are here.

"Do you want us to go?" I ask, wanting what he wants.

"No, no, no. Of course not. Why would you say that?" He asks, staring at me.

"Well, I can't tell if you are happy to see us. You were doing something really important, so I don't want to disrupt anything." I sit down at the bar and place my chin on my hand, resting my neck.

"Of course I'm happy to see you. I want you to come here whenever you want. This is your home if you want." He says smiling, "As for what I was doing before, it's not important. Don't worry. But I think I'm going to work on it in the office." He clears his throat, says goodbye to Johnny, and winks at me before stepping into Linda's old office and working on papers he didn't want me to see.

"John, go in the back and grab us both aprons and hats." I say to him.

"Okay," he smiles before skipping to the back of the bar.

When Johnny goes to the back, a few people start to walk in. When he doesn't come back, he starts to worry me. I start walking to the back.

"Johnny?" I call out, wanting to know where he was.

"Jon Jon, where are you?" I call out, busting through the back doors. He isn't there.

"Russ!" I call out, running towards Russell. I run into Linda's office saying,

"Russ, I can't find—"

Johnny is standing next to Russell in a little hat and child-sized apron.

"What is this?" I ask smiling, trying to cover up my panicking that I had just done a second ago.

"Russell made a custom hat and apron for me." He smiles.

"How do I look?" Johnny asks, while I stare at Russell. He looks back at me. I mouth a "thank you" at him because he has been better than what Cooper told me about.

Russell nods, shutting his eyes for a moment, as if saying, "you're welcome."

"Johnny, why don't you go start taking orders? Call me if there is any trouble." I say, still looking at Russell but this time with curious eyes.

"Okay." He runs out of the room.

"Walk, John!" I shout before he leaves.

"Yes, ma'am!" I get before turning my attention towards Russell.

"Why did you do that?" I ask him, crossing my arms with confusion.

"I thought it would be nice. Anyways, you guys are sticking around here for a while longer." He says, smirking at me.

"How would you know that?" I ask, watching him.

"John told me about your mother and you two going to visit your father. Why didn't you tell me about them?" He says, standing up out of his chair.

His plans for 'work' were still covered so that I couldn't see them. I am curious to see what kind of work he did and what he is trying to hide from me.

"I guess I am just embarrassed." I say, shrugging my shoulders while Russell advanced towards me.

"Look, I know they may seem like bad parents now, but they just made a few mistakes and they need forgiveness." He says, trying to help me fix things with my own parents.

"Russ, they aren't just bad parents. I can excuse my mother because she did take care of me for some of my life and she was there for some of it. But parents are supposed to be there for all of it. They are supposed to be your best friends when you don't have any.

"They are supposed to love you unconditionally even when you do something terribly wrong. But they never did, Russ. My dad killed Coop. I can't excuse that, ever. I'm sorry but I loved Cooper too much to do that to him. Even though Cooper forgives him." I say, shrugging my shoulders. People always cry. And people always leave. So right now, I am trying to stay and not cry, which is sort of new for me.

"I was a bad parent too. And so was Linda. But Cooper forgave us." Russ adds, putting his arm on my forearm. "But I'm not Cooper! He was so strong and he forgave more than I ever could." I say, clenching my jaw shut so I didn't cry.

"I know. But Cooper gained strength when he met you. He learned all of that strength from you. Because he didn't learn it from Linda or me. Listen Lorraine, he loved you and he would want you to fix things with your father. I know he would. I wasn't the best parent but I know what Cooper would've wanted. He'd want you to fix things with your father." He says, moving closer to me.

"I wish it was me instead of Cooper." I say, not realizing what came out of my mouth until it was too late. My brain thought it and it came out of my mouth. I couldn't stop it and I couldn't prevent it from coming out. So I ran.

I ran down the halls and up the stairs to where Linda was when she cried her eyes out about what Cooper said to her. Where she fell apart in front of me. And now all I wish is that I could fall apart in front of both of them. Just so that they could be here instead of somewhere else. I sob, not even trying to hold it in anymore. I stare at the skyline from up here and keep crying until it hurts my lungs. Even then, I keep crying.

"Take it easy." Russ says from behind me. I turn around and see his face. A similar face had been on Cooper. I pat the spot next to me and watch Russ sit down. I had stopped crying only when I touched his face.

"It's my fault." I say brushing my hands against the corners of the face Cooper had gotten his good looks from.

"Your son is gone and it's all my fault." I tear up but don't break down in front of him. I don't want to. I don't want him to see me weak. Taking a deep breath, I continue to trace the lines of his face with my hand.

"It's not your fault." Even his voice was similar.

"Your voice, your face, your hands," I say, holding up his hands that were even similar to Cooper's.

"Everything is so similar to him." I say, looking away from Russ to hold my head in my own hands.

"He really loved you. Even when I was pretending not to listen, I was dumbfounded about the way he talked about you. And now I see why. I thought that he had made up some beautiful woman but I was so wrong." Russ says, brushing his fingers against my cheek to wipe the tear off.

"I'm not here to tell you to be happy. I'm not here to tell you to stop being sad. Because that's really selfish. But you have to keep looking for positive things or we will all fall apart. We are all running on your strength, Lorraine. He was running on your strength. And he wouldn't stop talking about you. Jesus, I wanted to cover my ears with super glue." He makes me laugh.

"I fell in love with him." I choke out, my eyes glistening as I stare at the buildings across the street. Cookie-cutters. That's what they were. This building was different. A good different. A different that made it my favorite. Cooper made this place different. He made this place a totally different place. So did Linda. And now, they are gone. It is up to me and Russ to keep the bar up and the people coming in through the front door.

"I know you did." He says, wrapping his arm around my shoulders. I lean my head against Russ's shoulder, smiling.

"Did you seriously mean what you said the first time we met?" I say laughing, remembering the first time we met.

"Of course not. I knew the girl Cooper was hanging out with and a slut was not one word to describe her. The first time we met was definitely something though, wasn't it?" He asks me as I recall the first time we met.

"Russell Ross, Cooper's father." He holds out his hand. I shake it with a certain uneasiness about the way he is acting. He is perfectly fine with Cooper being gone. He doesn't blame Linda or anything by the looks of it.

"Pleasure to finally meet the man who gave Cooper nothing." I spit at him and walk away.

"Pleasure to meet you too, Miss Lorraine." My head snaps around as I walk away and I turn towards him slowly.

"How the hell do you know my name?" I slither at him as if I was a snake.

"Do you think I was that bad of a father that I didn't know who my son was hanging out with?" He asks, laughing.

"I do think you were a bad father for Cooper. He didn't get anything from you. All he got was bad mentalities and lessons that he wanted to teach to his future kids that he never got to create." I say, putting my hand on my hip and watching Cooper's father not even get uncomfortable.

"I'm surprised my son didn't do the deed and impregnate you, slut." He spits at me, smiling.

"Russell!" Linda shouts at her husband. I hate name-calling. Especially if it's the word, "slut." It's vile and poisonous, and I wish I could take it out of people's words towards me. It just makes me feel worse about myself.

"Don't worry, Linda. I can handle another horrible father." I eye Russell with my crystal eyes that turned to a black because of the darkness that was coming off of Russell.

"I loved your son. Even though you are a prick, he was an amazing person. Better than anything he learned from you. Linda is a better role model and she has blood all over her hands." I spit at him and then realize my mistake.

I laugh thinking of the names I called him and the names he called me. Now there isn't anybody I would trust more. Actually there is, but he's not here anymore. I guess I owe it to Cooper to trust Russell as well because he was his father and he never got the chance to bond with him. I let my worries run away as I lean against Russell's shoulder, the shoulder of my dead best friend's father. As I said, I let my worries run away. And then I remember Johnny.

****

CHAPTER 7:

"Johnny!" I run down the stair yelling.

"Lorraine, stop!" Russell tries to get a hold of me.

"I left Johnny!" I feel like the stupidest person in the world for leaving my five-year-old little brother behind while I cried like a baby up on the rooftop.

"Oh my God. I'm so stupid!" I yell, trying to get down the stairs in my boots as fast as possible.

"Lorraine, stop. You might fall." Russell says, trying to keep up with me. When we get to a landing, he grabs onto my waist and puts me back.

"John is fine. I called a friend of mine to watch him. He's fine." Russell says, holding my waist as I take a couple of deep breaths, trying to steady myself.

"Are you okay?" Russ asks me, staring into my eyes.

"I'm fine." I take a deep breath.

"I'm thinking about getting a stereo or stage so that we can play music or have an open mic night." Russ says, distracting me as we sit on the floor together, side by side.

"That would be cool." I say, breathless.

"And I am thinking about doing some construction, getting a bigger menu and different things like that. That's what I was working on." He says, as I finally find out what he was working on.

"Oh." I mumble, leaning against Russell for some air.

"Breathe." He says, putting a hand against my cheek. His arm is caught around my waist because the wall and my body are keeping him from getting his arm out. I take a deep breath and move to stand up.

"Here, let me." Russ says, getting up and holding out his hands for me. I take them, graciously. His strength sent me barreling into his chest. My face collides with his chest and all I do is laugh. Russell catches my waist once again and holds it. I could feel the heat rise to my chest only because this exact moment had happened with his son and it felt too destructive to have it be substituted with his father.

"Are you okay?" He chuckles.

"I'm fine." I hold my nose because it hurts a little bit.

"Come on," he says holding my waist, which is kind of uncomfortable because he is way older than me, but it is kind of nice to have someone there. He was acting like my father figure and for once, it felt good to have a father there, even if it wasn't my own.

****

When I get down stairs, I watch as Johnny and a man I have never met, serve people together, making a pretty good team.

"Hey, little man." Russell says, running over to Johnny, who is cleaning up a table. I smile at the two of them together as I place my hands behind my back to straighten it.

"Hi, I'm David Lovett." The man comes up to me and holds out his hand with a smile.

"Lorraine Lowry, Cooper's friend." I say, removing my hand to shake his before putting it back.

"My sister is Cooper's mother." David says, smiling back, happily instead of being sad that both of them are dead.

"I met her." I say, nodding as he gives me a skeptical look because she's been dead for so long. I clear my throat and thank him for watching Johnny.

"Oh, it was no problem. I was actually looking for something proactive to do. I just didn't think it would be watching a kid and serving at Russ's place." He says with a laugh. I join in with him while watching Johnny and Russell get to work.

"Well, you've been released from duty. I owe you big time, Mr. Lovett." I say, shaking his hand again.

"I think I'm going to stick around a while longer, if that's alright with you. I always liked this place." He says, smiling at the environment in *Billy's Bar*, his hands in his pockets.

"We are thinking about adding a stage and or a stereo in here. You know, adding music or an open mic night. Just something new for the place, you know?" I say, crossing my arms and imagining the stage or the stereos in our *Billy's*. Our *Billy's*. I like the sound of that.

"Laura first opened this place in memory of our father. She wanted to commemorate him somehow and what better way then working for him every day?" He says, smirking at the thought of his sister. Originally, I always assumed the bar was Linda's but now that I knew it was Laura's and Linda was keeping her memory alive for the sake of Cooper, I could feel the ragging sensation deep in my chest. Oh Linda, why did you go?

"She's just beautiful." I say, looking at his face.

"Yeah. She was." He says, staring at the people as they ate and not worrying about anything.

"You don't mind if we do some construction on the place, right? We are planning on making it better." I say, hoping he says yes.

"Of course. If there is anything my sister would want more, it's for this place to get used more. Change the name for all I care. As long as it runs in the family, I don't care what anybody does with it." He says, moving with me to where the hats and the aprons were hanging. He considered me family? I hand him a set.

"Let's get to work before Russell kills me for standing around and talking." I smirk.

"Alright." He slips the hat on his head and smiles at me.

"Lorraine! Get your butt out here!" Russell yells from inside the bar. I laugh and look at David.

"Yeah, Lorraine! Help us out!" Johnny yells just like Russ.

"That a boy, John." I hear Russ say.

"Hey, don't corrupt my brother." I say to Russ, who is now within my eye view. I walk to where Russ is cooking on the grill.

"You better not be corrupting my little one." I say, shoving a finger in his face.

"Oh, yeah?" Russell says moving closer to me, his hands open wide, shaking with fake fear. Standing in the center of the bar with that same smirk on his face, I felt as if Cooper was standing with me.

"Oh, yeah." I say, smirking before exiting the area where Russell is.

"Or else." I mutter, but I know he hears me for moments later, arms wrap around my waist and lift me off the floor.

"Russell, put me down!" I say while I felt my whole body shake with laughter against Russell's.

Russell puts me down and sends me off to work. I just can't help thinking that he was flirting with me and I don't want him to. He is like a father to me, after all. What do I do, Cooper?

****

I sit down at the bar, sighing, watching my brother turn the open sign to closed. It is roughly eight or nine. I don't have a watch on me. Russ parks down next to me, leaning on his elbows that are against the bar.

"You should stop by the house tomorrow. I want to give you some of Cooper's things. I just don't know what you want. But he would want that." He says, nodding.

"Okay. I could actually stop off tonight if you want." I let him know, wanting Johnny to fall asleep on the ride there.

"Sure." He smiles brightly at me.

"Do you want help packing away his room and Linda's?" I ask, knowing this must be hard for him to do.

"I would really like that." Russ says, staring at me before I turn away, smiling at him, and take Johnny with me to our car.

After arriving at Russell's mansion, I park and stare at my sleeping baby brother in the backseat. He has had a rough, not-so-lonely day. I call Russell's house number, not knowing his cell number.

"Hello?" Russ says, picking up the phone rather quickly. His voice sounds deeper on the telephone.

"Hey, Russ. I'm outside but Johnny fell asleep and I don't want to leave him alone." I say, fiddling with the steering wheel.

"Okay. I'm coming out now." He says, before letting the line go dead. A few seconds later, he is at my door, grinning. I point towards the backseat before putting a finger over my mouth, telling him to be quiet. He keeps smiling and advances toward our car.

Open the door, he mouths in the front window. I unlock the car and let Russ open John's door. He unbuckles him slowly and carefully, and takes Jon Jon in his arms. I half-open the front door, letting the boys walk in the house first but Russ has other plans. Even with a five-year-old kid in his hands, he is still a gentleman. He stands, gesturing his hand for me to go. I say, "Thank you," before walking inside, now holding open the door. Russ leads me upstairs to a bedroom that says, "Cooper's Room, Keep Out!" on the front door. I smile as Russ tucks Johnny away in the sheets.

"I don't know exactly what you want, so feel free to roam

the room and take whatever you please." He says, before

walking out of the room.

"Thank you, Russ!" I say, before he leaves. He smiles his

big old smile at me and leaves me alone in my best

friend's room.

****

After what felt like hours of looking through

Cooper's room, I finally finish with two boxes of things. I

basically took drawings that he did of me but never

showed me, his hat and apron from Billy's, his

headphones, his iPod with all his wacky music, his record

player and some of his records, more drawing books that

were filled with his artwork, a menu for the bar I found in

his room with new dishes and ideas for it, and an old dog

tag he used to wear with his name, *"Cooper Allen Lovett-*

Ross," printed across it. I walk down the stairs and into

the kitchen, finding Russell cooking something on the

stovetop.

"Hi." I say, sitting down at the counter that had high chairs behind it.

"Did you finish?" Russ asks, smiling at me, while ignoring the food that is burning behind him. I ignore his stares and walk over to cook the food behind him while he looks at me the whole time. I sleep in Cooper's room that night because even though nobody could see it, I am still grieving the loss of "*Cooper Allen Lovett-Ross*," my best friend.

****

FIRST DAY GOING BACK TO SCHOOL SINCE COOPER DIED:

All I receive is stares. That's all I had ever received but this time, it is worse. The stares eat me alive everywhere I go because I missed a couple of days of school. Moments like these are the ones that make me hate my life. Moments like these are the ones that destroy me. Completely and utterly. How do I fix these stares, Cooper? I know he would say, "Just let them keep staring at how beautiful and strong you are." But that's trash. That's just complete bullshit. In fact, I think my brother could give me better advice than that. And he's five-years-old. School is never the place I did extremely well in for two reasons:

One, I am different.

And two, people hate a different that they can't copy. Teenagers love followers. Teens in my school are all followers. But only the rare ones are actually different, like me. Most of their divergent spirits die and they become as bland as everyone else. But only some people stay the same, like me. My grades are so high that they could kill you. People like me focus on our grades so that we don't focus on the staring or the social life that some people could dream about for the rest of their life but never get it.

Then, there are the people with social lives, who don't usually have grades at all because they are so concerned about beer pong and about who had sex with who, that they might not even get into a college to learn and work to live. Or there are some people who just dream of having a social life while having good grades. That's where the people like me come in, once again. It's pretty bullshit that you can't have both.

I don't focus on my social life at all or the staring that always comes my way. I focus on the number in my head. FOUR. That is my GPA. And that's what I am focusing on. Because if I don't, who knows where my mind would be at? This morning, I woke up late and woke up at Cooper's house; a double no-no. I was horribly late to school, I missed all of first period, and couldn't drop Johnny off to school. Thank goodness Russ offered to take him and I am truly grateful for that, even with all his staring. I like Johnny and Russell spending time together. I would have liked Cooper and Johnny to have spent time together but I couldn't do anything about that. He is gone and he isn't coming back.

****

I make it through the end of the day without crying, without thinking, and without smiling. As I make my way to my locker, I notice a person standing there.

Lucas James Kelly, my ex-star-crossed lover.

"What the hell do you want, Luke?" I say, opening my locker.

"Okay, I must have been high the day we talked because I don't remember a thing about what I said but I know that all of it wasn't true. What did I say?" Lucas says, knowing that whatever he said is probably half true.

"You know you were always bad in crisis and bad in a situation like this." I say, smirking remembering the day he said, "I Love You," to me.

"Okay. Can I help you?" I ask, not looking at him.

"Look at—" His famous line was relaying in my head over and over again.

"NO." I say pretty loudly without realizing it and turn to walk down the hall opposite way, slamming the locker as I left.

"Lorraine, why?" He asks, holding my forearm.

I shook him off and said, "You should be asking yourself that question. You broke up with me." I snicker and walk away with guilt for making the boy who broke my heart feel like crap. I should be the one feeling like crap because I still continue to put the pieces back in his hands, hoping that he will fix me. But he won't because he's not mine anymore. And he doesn't realize but he never will be again. I can guarantee that. At least, I think I can.

"Lorraine, come on. Just talk to me like a person." He says grabbing my forearm again.

"What the hell would you even want to talk about, Lucas? There is nothing to say. It's over. You said it pretty clear when you broke up with me. I don't need for there to be a second time, especially if it's in public." I say shaking my arm out of his grip and walking back down the halls. Lucas pulls me into the classroom on his right without my consent.

"What the hell—" I yell before Lucas covers my mouth and pulls me back against him, covering the door.

"Get the hell off of me!" I scream, getting out of his grip.

"You can't do this and then expect me to not care, Lucas. You broke up with me. This is freaking nuts." I put my head in my hands and sit down in one of the desks.

"Listen, Lorraine. I'm trying to make it better between us. I really am. I didn't want to break up with you." He says kneeling down beside the desk I am sitting at.

"Are you high?" I ask him the legitimate question.

"No. I'm serious. Lorraine, I love you so much." He says for the first time ever, grabbing my hand on one knee.

"Lucas, you can't do this to me." I say holding my head, my eyesight getting foggy from tears once again like the first day.

"Lorraine, we can fix this. Just help me get rid of April." He continues to hold my hand.

"Stop embarrassing yourself, Lucas." I say turning away and biting my lip to avoid a sudden breakdown.

"I know you love me too. You have to. I still see the way you look at me, Lorraine. Tell me you don't feel that." He puts my hand against his chest, to touch his heart.

"Stop." I whisper, suddenly breaking down.

"Oh, Lorraine. I'm going to make it better." He holds my head and brings it closer to his chest.

"Cooper..." I whisper wrapping my arms around Cooper. I look up and see Lucas instead. I push Lucas back and hold my hand against my mouth, in shock. I need Cooper.

Sometimes when you go through something really bad, as heartbreak, you latch onto someone for guidance and reassurance so that you can move forward. And in that moment, that person is the best thing in your life. Cooper is the best thing in my life right now.

"Cooper? Who's Cooper?" Lucas steps back after I push him away from me.

"Someone who would never make the same mistakes you keep on making." I get up out of my seat.

"Listen, Lorraine. I love you." Lucas says, advancing towards me. My instincts kick in and all of a sudden, my hand shoots out, smacking Luke across the face.

"I-I'm so sorry." I say sobbing into my hand before drawing in a deep breath. "You just don't get to say that."

"But it's true." He says moving closer to me. I want to run out of this room but I know I have to stay and finish this conversation or I would forever regret it.

"Luke, this isn't the Notebook because I clearly don't like you back anymore." I say pulling his hands off of mine. Putting my leg over my left leg and placing my elbow on *my thigh to support my head on my hand, I laugh inside at how weird this situation is.*

Luke doesn't say a word. He just quickly exits the room, leaving me with nothing but my crowded thoughts and my mind that is filled with chaos, just like my world.

"Oh my gosh." He says, rubbing the back of his neck, hitting the locker in front of him in the process.

"Watch it. That's my locker." I say, smirking at his embarrassment around me now.

"Is there any way I can convince you that what I said wasn't true?" He asks me, with his eyebrows furrowed.

"Nope." I pop the 'p.'

"Alright, who are you going to tell?" He asks me, watching my facial expressions. I take a step back.

"Do you even know me, Luke? Because if you knew me, you would know I wouldn't tell anyone something like that. The thought that you would even think that I would tell someone is mind-boggling." I say, opening my locker and shaking him off like a tick.

"I'm sorry. I just—I've been very out of it lately. She's becoming obsessive." He says, whispering about his new girlfriend, who is eyeing us right now with her big stink eye.

I turn around and wave to April with my fingers, only moving the tops of them like they do in movies. Lucas grabs my hands and laughs while I join in. Then, we realize how close we are and I back away.

"Look, I'm sorry about hurting you. It really was all my fault." He says, fiddling with his hands in front of him.

"It's okay, I guess. I didn't mean to get really mad a couple of minutes ago. I'm just going through a rough time right now." I say, tucking my hair covering my face behind my ears.

"What happened to you? You miss a couple of days of school and come back like you're a completely different person. Everybody can see it. That's why there is so much staring." He says, shaping his pointer finger and thumb into circles and putting them on his eyes. I laugh easily because of the stupid things like this that he does that made me fall for him.

"I just—remember when I said something about Cooper? When I mentioned Cooper, you flipped. Do you remember that?" He nods a little before I continue.

"Well, I only knew him for a really short while but he became my best friend. Okay? And he saved my life by taking a knife for me." I look away.

"Holy smokes, Lorraine. Are you okay?" Lucas moves his hands to my shoulders so that he could turn my body around to stare into my eyes.

"Not really. I mean I'm doing a good job of saving everybody from the pain that they have from Cooper being gone but nobody's there to save me, you know?" I say, wanting more than anything to get out of the school right now and away from Lucas.

"It's okay." Lucas slowly brings me into his strong arms and his warm chest that I had secretly missed so much. But something still felt incredibly wrong. Was it because I knew what Cooper's chest felt like?

"It's not." I say, as Lucas puts his chin down on my head and rests it there while he holds me tight.

I have a theory. Though people leave your life for good reasons, I think that people don't always leave. I think that people have reasons to leave and when they do, yes it's pretty bad on you, but I think that when they come back, it's the best part. Like in movies. Let's say the Notebook. She has a choice: she can either marry the rich dude that she loves or she can marry the poor guy, who makes her happy and who she loves very much. I mean, the poor dude built a dream house for her.

All philosophers think love is a terrible feeling. "Love is a serious mental disease," Plato had said. "It is impossible to love and be wise," said Francis Bacon, who was an English Philosopher. "Love has reasons which reason cannot understand," which is a controversial quote by Blaise Pascal, a French Mathematician. I think that love is something different.

I think love is to know someone's failures, stupidities, and ugly spots in life and still see a perfect person. You see, if you truly love someone, you don't look past their differences or the things that make them unique. You cherish them because they are themselves and you are you. To love is to see perfection in the imperfection. It is to not wish for someone to be different but just praying that they stay the same. Sometimes, people never find that; people don't find love in their whole lives. They are the lonely ones who will try to break your love apart and make you suffer what they have suffered. So when you find love, you must never let it go. You find it and hold onto it.

Just like Cooper, you don't know how much time you have left with a person. So I held onto Lucas James Kelly, the boy who broke my heart and is now trying to fix a different broken heart; a broken heart due to death. I am not trying to understand love. Love is not comprehendible. Understanding love is something that nobody has figured out yet. And the probability is that no one ever will be able to understand love. No philosopher or mathematician. No one. Not even a person like Luke or I.

Experiencing love is what life is all about. It's why we are here, to find love and hold onto it for as long as we can. It's what we are trained to do as humans, to love and to be loved. When you love, you know that somewhere along the lines you could get your heart broken. Love anyways. When you are loved, you know that person can get their heart broken; choose to love anyways. It's all about love. It's all about finding someone to share life with. It's not about how many drinks you can take or about how many drugs you can smoke without passing out or getting completely trashed; it's about love. So when I walk through the hallways, I am the one winning while everybody else is staring. Because I have found love but I've lost it too. But now, I found a new love, an old love. And I have to love with courage because I know my heart could be broken once again.

****

I laugh. For the first time in a while, I laugh uncontrollably. I shake and wobble because I'm laughing and I'm happy right now; I'm happy when I'm with Lucas. He's walking me to my car and I can feel the sweat start pilling down my back, my voice start to get heavy because I have no idea what to say or do next. Maybe he still 'loved' me; maybe he has no idea what the hell love is. When silence fades over our conversation, I speak up.

"Do you want to come over? I could make some dinner and I know Johnny would be happy to see you." I say, smiling, not trying to make things awkward by inviting him over but slightly wanting him to come over. Sometimes, even after a harsh breakup, you can like your ex. That's when it usually goes to utter shit.

"Sure. I'd like that a lot." He smiles back.

"Cool. So I'm going to go." I gesture to the blue car behind me, my key located in my hand.

"Okay. Be safe."

"You too. Thanks for walking me to my car." I say, before getting in my car and watching him watch me drive away.

****

"Hey, little buddy." I say as Johnny runs over to me from a long day of school.

"Hi, Lorraine."

"What's up?" I ask as we walk to the car together, hand in hand.

"Nothing much." A blush crawls excitedly on his face.

"Alright, who's the girl?" I question, watching his facial reactions. I couldn't believe my baby brother has a crush.

"Her name is Lucy. She's in my grade and she's beautiful." He closes his eyes and imagines her as if he hasn't seen her in centuries.

"Whoa. Slow your roll, buddy. You can't jump all over the poor girl." I laugh at his sudden burst of a little crush.

There are more things to fawn over than a simple crush. Oh, if he only knew.

"Sorry." He gets in the car and buckles himself.

"Hey, buddy. Is it alright with you if Lucas comes over?" I don't want to bring up strong feelings that Johnny had for Lucas, not wanting him to get attached again.

"Are you two a couple again?" Johnny leans over to me, against the seatbelt, pressing to know the answer with anticipation beating red on his face.

"Calm down, buddy. No, we aren't, but he's coming over tonight and he's going to have dinner with us. We are friends." I make it clear that we aren't a couple.

"Yes!" He pumps his fists in the air, childishly.

"This is the best day ever!" He exclaims.

"Okay, calm down or I'm going to have to tell Lucas to stay home." I glance at him, continuing to drive towards our home.

****

When we get home, Luke is sitting right on the front steps of our house.

"I'm so sorry for making you wait. I had to pick up Johnny." I gesture to the crazy kid in the back of the car, who is trying to get out, bolting as fast as he can. He hugs Lucas, who is astonished at how much Johnny has missed him. I huff before walking to the door, unlocking it, shutting the alarm off, and locking the car.

"Boys, wash your hands and you can go play." I take the hair tie off my wrist, tying my hair back. Sitting down at the table, I start to do my homework while the boys run upstairs like five-year-olds, which I can't blame Johnny for. I hear the door slam and I smirk before starting my math homework. As I keep doing my homework, finishing one thing after the other, the boys eventually come back down stairs, Johnny begging for dinner soon.

"What do you boys want for dinner?" I rub my hands together. I have a couple of sentences left to write in an essay and then, I will be free.

"Can we have something special? It's a special occasion." He bounces up and down.

"What's the special occasion?" I ask, Johnny curiously, turning my head in my chair toward him.

"You and Lucas became friends again." He smiles at the both of us. I stare up at Lucas with apprehension locked in my eyes.

"I could celebrate to that." I shrug my shoulders as Lucas answers back, "Of course. We are such good friends now.

Aren't we, Lorri?" He asks me, putting an arm around my shoulders.

"We sure are, James." I say, calling him by his middle name which he loved, putting my arm around his waist. We aren't that good friends, I mean we just made up today, but I'm assuming it is a joke.

"I guess I'll run out to the store then." I grab my purse on the back of my chair.

"We'll come with you." Lucas says, grabbing his shoes by the doorway.

"Luke. What are you doing, man? We got the whole house to ourselves." Johnny walks over to where Lucas is sitting, tying his laces.

"Dude, we've got to go help your sister. She's getting the food that is going in your tummy." Luke tickles Johnny.

"Fine." Johnny pushes away Luke's hands with a smirk, slipping on his little shoes.

"Ready, boys?" I call from the kitchen. Quickly finishing my essay, I put away my things that are scattered across the table, while they get ready to make a quick trip to the supermarket.

"Yep." Lucas takes Johnny's hand and waits for me outside. Turning on the alarm on, I lock the door behind me before getting in the car with the boys. Lucas sits in the front seat with me while Johnny is in the back seat, sitting in the middle with his car seat.

"Let's go." I smile as we pull away towards the grocery store.

****

"Alright; Lucas, you are on cart duty. Johnny, you are on the job of grabbing the things we need and putting them in the cart. If you can't reach, Luke'll help you out." I know we need to move quickly because tonight, it is busy. Though it is a Monday night and it doesn't look busy at all, it is still busy in my mind.

"Well, what are you going to do?" Johnny asks me, holding Lucas's hand.

"I am going to be concentrating on what we need." I pull up a recipe for Johnny's favorite dish, Chicken Parmesan.

"Okay, first thing is first. Chicken." We start to walk down the aisles into the meat areas.

"I need boneless chicken." I search the meat freezers; when I find the meat, I hand it to Johnny and he puts it in the cart. As I stand there and read about what else I need, Lucas laces his hand that wasn't holding Johnny's, in mine. I don't mind at all. After all, we are friends. And as we walk together with Johnny by our sides like a little family, I thought about how holding hands is completely *not* a friendly gesture. It is a *loving* gesture. But hey, I was down for that too. I was keeping my options open, like Cooper told me to do.

****

When we arrive home, the boys brought the bags in for me and laid all the ingredients on the table.

"Okay, you can go play. Thank you for your help." I watch Johnny climb the stairs on his own.

"Luke, aren't you coming?" He turns around now that he doesn't see Lucas behind him.

"In a minute, buddy. I think I'm going to help your sister a little bit." He stares into my eyes with amazement. It isn't only making me thrash under his gaze, it is making my cheeks grow red.

"Okay." Johnny giggles and brings himself upstairs to give us some space.

I smile before moving over to the kitchen sink to wash my hands. He stands close behind me; so close I can feel his tepid breath on my neck. I lean back, getting a paper towel to wipe my hands. His hands clutch to my hips snuggly and suddenly, I'm turned around facing him. His eyes are locked on mine and his hands firm on my hips, when, without a second of thought, I pull his neck down to mine and we tie our lips together.

His hands move harshly up and down my back with fierce movements. I suck in a breath through my nose and pull him closer, pressing my body against his in the process. His hands lift me up and place my butt down lightly on the counter. I watch him as he kisses down my neck and back up slowly, making every kiss count. I am out of breath by the time I realize that we need to stop.

"Luke, we have to stop. This is wrong." I breathlessly say.

He looks up and flashes his eyes down to my lips. "You don't know how long I have waited for that."

"We shouldn't have done that. Aren't we keeping it at friends? I've got to make dinner for Johnny." I smirk before he helps me off the counter, his hands still around my hips after I'm on my own two feet.

"It's not wrong if you liked it too." He smirks. I'll admit, I loved it, but I wasn't going to give him that.

"It was okay." I offer, smirking while he says, "Can I get one more kiss?"

He breaks out into a smile as I lean in towards him but before our lips meet, I pull back and tease him. I walk away towards the kitchen table to sort out the ingredients, but before I can do that, his hands latch onto my hips and he pulls me back in his arms for one last kiss, the one I didn't give him. Our lips meet harshly but it still feels good to kiss someone who isn't all in my head like Cooper had been in my coma dream.

"Better?" I walk out of his arms towards the table again, putting away the things that need to be kept in the fridge and start making the chicken.

"You need help?"

"You can help me make the chicken right now." I show him how to season the meat and then drench it in egg before breading it and placing it in the frying pan. After it's fried, we put it in a pan and put the mozzarella, parmesan cheese, and sauce that I made by hand while Luke tries to fry the rest of the chicken. And when I say try, I mean try. He could not fry anything without getting burned. I would say he got burned about five times before the first piece of chicken was finished. When the chicken came out of the oven, I wanted to eat it right away because of how beautiful it glowed.

"We did a hell of a job." I say to Luke, who is staring at the chicken instead of me this time.

"Can I eat it now?" Luke asks, advancing closer to it.

"You can if you want to get burned another time. This time, the burn will be inside your mouth." I laugh at him as he steps back from the chicken.

"We have to wait for it to cool off." I place the chicken on a special plate that we only used for Johnny's chicken parmesan. He is so specific with his favorite foods. He has to have them a certain way.

"Johnny! Food is ready!" I tell him and then say, "Shoot!"

"What happened?" Luke asks, coming up behind me after placing the food on the table.

"I forgot to make his favorite dessert!" I hold my head in my hands.

"What's his favorite dessert?" Luke moves closer to my stressed being.

"Brownies." I move to the cabinet to see if I have a box of brownies I could make and staring me in the face is the biggest bug I have ever seen in my life. I scream louder than I ever have and bolt to the living room.

"What the hell happened?" Luke joins me in the next room to question what happened. I'm standing on our couch, terrified, holding a pillow. I HATE BUGS. I despise them in every way possible and I wish that bugs never existed.

"There's a bug!" I point toward in the kitchen. Luke smiles lightly before coming over and letting me climb on his back. We walk into the kitchen slowly and I clutch his neck tightly.

"I can't breathe, Lorraine." His strained voice says it all. I am holding on way too tightly.

"Sorry." I let go of my tight grasp on his neck and put my head in the crook of his neck while he checks where the bug went. I see that the bug is still in the cabinet, staring up at us.

"Get rid of it." I hide my face in Lucas's neck, my legs clutching him even tighter at the sight of the pest.

"Alright." He drops me and grabs my laptop off the counter and uses his hand to move the bug onto the device. He cups his hand around the bug so it can't fly in the house and scare the crap out of me and slowly, he places the bug outside my front door, off the device. When he comes back inside, I kiss him. Not on the cheek, cutely. Not on the neck, passionately. I kiss him on the lips because I thought what he did was not only magnificent, but chivalrous and oddly romantic. I smile and pull away, moving to make the brownies.

By the time Johnny comes down, the brownies are in the oven, and cooking like nothing ever happened. We sit down at the table nicely, for once. With our mother getting better, our father gone, and with Luke back in the picture, I am happy. I think this happiness could last for a lifetime.

****

When dinner is over, I ask Johnny to help me do the dishes while I ask James to get the boxes in the back of my car for me. The boxes of things I took from Cooper's room. When he brings them in, he asks me, "What is all of this?"

"It's some stuff from Cooper's house." I know that he knew of Cooper from when I mentioned him I told him about how he was a close friend when Luke hadn't been.

"Oh," is all he says before moving the boxes up to my room.

"Luke, when you go up, can you bring my laptop up? I need that for later." I think out loud for the most part. He glares at me, oddly.

"What? I write on it." I share with him something that I've never shared with anyone but Cooper, who wasn't here anymore.

He nods and asks me with a smirk on his face, "Did you ever meet Kelly2651?"

I turn around, unsteady, not ready for the truth that has slapped me in the face so many times. I was clueless.

"That was you?" I bite my lip. He nods, smiling at me. My lip quivers and tears start forming in my eyes.

"How did you even know about my blog?" My eyes water at the thought that though Lucas was not there, he was watching after me.

"Katherine told me about it." He shrugs. And then it hits me. Katherine; Kitty. We used to call her Kitty when she was little. I should've known.

"Luke, I need you to watch Johnny for a couple of minutes. Take the brownies out when they are done and use a kitchen towel to take them out so you don't burn yourself. Thanks!" I quickly grab my purse, barking instructions before giving him a kiss, and running out the door. I lock it behind me and run into my car, heading straight for Katherine's house.

****

Brandon answers the door.

"I need to see your sister." I move past him and up the stairs.

"Hello to you, too." Brandon smirks from behind me.

"I can't believe you are going to the army." I shake my head, opening her door, and not seeing Katherine in her room.

"Where is she?"

"She went to some party." He shrugs his shoulders.

"How did you know I'm going into the army?" He itches the back of his neck.

Katherine didn't go to parties. Her and I used to miss the parties we were invited to just because. Even though Katherine is a lot different than me, parties just weren't her thing. I don't wait for an answer. I get my phone out and track her phone. She is at the bridge we used to go to as kids. It has always had a breathtaking view over the ocean. We used to spend most of our times just looking over the ocean, smiling at each other because in that moment, we were satisfied.

I get in the car quickly and drive less than five minutes to reach the bridge. I pull over on the side of the highway and see Katherine's car on the side of the road. I watch as Katherine stands on the edge of the bridge, her arms, latching onto the sides of the bridge. The sky hits the ocean at the horizon line while the sun locks the both and saves them from clashing with each other.

"Katherine!" I scream, wondering what the hell she is doing. I see her head turn and her eyes lock on mine. Immediately, she starts crying and shaking her head no.

"Katherine, get back on the bridge." I slowly move closer to her so that now, we are only a couple of meters apart.

"Stay back." She lets her hands go and balances on the ledge of the bridge.

"Katherine, I came to say I'm sorry. I have to say I'm sorry. For what I said that day you asked me what happened, for what I did when you tried to talk to me. I'm so sorry for it all." Tears clutch the edge of my cheek bones as they slide.

"You can't say that out of pity, Lorraine. It doesn't work that way." She snarls at me through her clenched jaw.

"Look, Kat. I'm not doing this out of pity. I'm not here out of pity. I'm here because I'm sorry for everything you had to go through without me. I'm sorry because I know going through your friends leaving you must've been hard and I'm sorry that you had to survive your mother and father's divorce on your own. I should've been there to help you decide where you want to live and I swear if I was there, I would just force you to live with me. I'm sorry that I couldn't have been there when your brother told you he is going into the army. I'm so fucking sorry, Katherine. It's my fault you are standing up there." I move closer slowly.

"No. Don't say sorry. I am a bad friend. I should have worried more about you than my popularity. I hate my life!" She screams, looking at the water.

"Don't hate your life. Because I think it's a pretty good one. Listen, one of my friends recently died and he didn't choose it. Don't choose death. It chooses us sometimes and that's unfair but people shouldn't choose death. Life is good, I promise. Take my hand and I'll show you, Katherine. Make up for the time we lost. Because if you go, then so do I." I hold my hand out moving closer.

"Stop moving closer." She backs up on the ledge, facing me. Her foot misses a step and she goes from standing on the ledge, to slipping off of it.

"Katherine!" I yelp, running over to help her. She looks like a frightened girl, scared of the world, and she is. Someone has to save her from it because her parents aren't going to her brother isn't going to, and her friends aren't going to.

"Just hold on," I tell her before rolling up my sleeves and bending down to reach my hands out.

"Grab my hand." I hold it out towards her as an offering gesture, a gesture that would foreshadow our future.

"Why should I?" She asks, frightened but still standing by her beliefs when she got up on this bridge.

"Because this time, I won't let go. I promise." I reach out for her hand again with a serious expression on my face. When she got the big picture, she took my hand and allowed me to pull her to safety on the other side of the bridge.

"Listen, I don't have all the words to make it better but I do have my shoulders for you to cry on whenever you need and I do have the arms to hold you up when you can't hold yourself, okay? And for as long as you need it, my house is your house." I walk her to her car.

"Follow me back to my house. I promise everything will be okay this time, Kat. Come on, I have Lucas back at my house with Johnny." I smile at her with hope gleaming through my voice. She sends me a reassuring smile back as she climbs in her driver's side. She follows me all the way home, safely.

"Come on, I promise that you won't have to go through any of this alone." I put my arm around her shoulders as we walk through my front door.

"We're home!" I smile, brightly.

"Thank you." She wipes away some tears that escaped her eyes.

"Hey, that's what friends are for." I hug her tightly before watching Lucas pop out from the door. His eyes brighten right away and I think you could tell that we would live somewhat close to happily ever after, just like Cooper told me he wanted.

****

4 YEARS LATER...

"Johnny! Let's go! We have to pick up Mom!" I yell up the stairs to him. He comes bolting down quickly, slipping on his shoes fast when he reaches the front door.

"Ready." He smirks his childish smirk, except he isn't much of a child anymore. Johnny is now a bright nine-year-old, who keeps getting on my nerves. He is becoming such a man that I can't take it.

"Luke, we are going to be late, honey! I told them I would be there nine o'clock sharp." I slip on my heels. Lucas moved in with us on the day we rekindled, his parents not caring where he went anymore. Katherine moved in as well, who is probably still upstairs sleeping, which reminds me:

"Katherine!" I scream, piercing the whole house.

"I'M UP!" She screams coming down the stairs, fully dressed, glasses sitting on her nose.

"You didn't put in your contacts?" I ask her, smirking.

"You are lucky I even got up." She itches her head with sleep on her eyelids.

"Lucas, honey! We are going to be late!" I yell again, because he is seriously taking forever.

"I'm coming. Just putting on my shoes." I walk back to the front door.

"You guys go on out. Lucas is driving." I push them out of the house. I have to get out of here and on time.

"Luke, I'm going to have to leave without—" Lucas comes out of our room and down the stairs with a bouquet of flowers.

"What's all this for?" I ask, smiling. I know what it is for obviously. I am just playing him.

"Don't tell me you forgot. It's our anniversary." His smile fades.

"Of course I didn't forget." I shine at him, before hugging him. I put the flowers in water before turning the alarm on and walking out the door, hand in hand with Lucas.

****

When we arrive there, my mother is waiting out front with a nurse. Our mother looks totally different without all the dye in her hair. She has white hair now, though she only aged four years in the last time we saw her with her full head of black hair. Our mother still looked beautiful though, a different type of beautiful. A *better* type of beautiful. I get out of the passenger side quickly and run up to my mother.

"Mom," I gasp before wrapping my arms around her. In all truth, I missed my mother, even though in the past, she has done some pretty bad things. You can't hate your mother. She kept you inside her stomach for nine freaking months and then she ruined her body just to push you out. You can't hate your mother. Unless she killed someone like my father did. Then you can hate whoever the hell you want.

"I missed you." I let her know as she smiles naturally.

"I feel much better." She says, breathing a fresh breath of air, instead of one filled with alcohol.

"You look much better. Let's get you home." I take her suitcase from her to throw in the back.

"Here. Let me get that." Luke gets out of the car to take the suitcase from me. He puts it in the back for me and I smile at him, pecking his lips before we pull away with my mother in the back seat.

"Mom, I have to get to work but I'll talk to you later. Will you be okay here? Do you want to come?" I ask, worried that she might do something rash here by herself. Everyone comes to the restaurant with me. It's a family business, after all.

"Sure, I'll go." We all stay in the car and drive off to the restaurant, where my life took place and is still taking place.

****

We pull up to *Cooper's Cafe*, a new and improved *Billy's Bar*. The bar took away from the mistakes and the problems that happened here. The bar made people forget. We didn't want to forget. We wanted to heal and we thought that instead of a bar, let's have a cafe. And that's exactly what we did. So we named it after Cooper. He inspired the menu, after all. He wrote it himself in his room. He even designed the cover. We put it on paper but he inspired all of it. He's been the inspiration forever.

I am now a junior in college and cannot wait to graduate. Luke has recently finished college with a business degree. He handles all the financial business and sometimes, even helps out at the cafe. I'm getting my degree in literature. Cooper told me to follow my dreams and I have. I wish he could have followed his. I walk into my second home and shout, "Russ!"

Russell pops out from behind the wall and smiles. Russell now has some serious white hair, just like my mother, but his smile has never changed.

"Lorraine, how's it going?" Russell signed the cafe over to us about a year ago because he felt that we should keep it in the family. I cried because he considered me family. I guess we've been through too much not to be family. I walk up to Russ and hug him. It's my routine every day. I hug Russell before every day starts. Linda and Cooper would be so proud of him and who he's become, even after everything that he went through.

"Let's get to work." Johnny says, walking toward the front door to turn the sign to open like he did a couple of years back.

Katherine gets in the back to do the cooking like she has for the past four years, Luke grabs a hat and apron for both him, Johnny, and my mother, as I slide on Cooper's hat and apron every single day. Sometimes, I even slide on his dog tag. Luke understands that I miss him sometimes. I mean, I lost Cooper Allen Ross. It is obviously a great loss. I don't want to pretend when I'm around Luke.

I want it to be the real thing or nothing at all, just like it was with me and Cooper. And it is. He understands me, I understand him, and for the first time, I think I could spend the rest of my life like this, because it's not that bad. It's better because Cooper made it better. It's better because now, all these people are in my life and it's all better. Who ever said, "It gets better," is so right. So what? The road may have a few bumps and you may get a few bruises. The ending result is totally worth the huge trip to get there.

"Luke, I need you to help me out at table 4." I kiss him on his way to table 4.

"I love our anniversary." He says, smirking at me before attending to table 4.

"I love you," I shout after him before walking into the back. I am planning on setting up a special date here at Cooper's for Luke and I.

"Kat, are you going to help me out later?" I see Katherine flipping burgers.

"Of course. I think what you are doing is adorable. But I think what he is doing for you is so cute." She jumps up and down before getting back to her collection of burgers that needed flipping. I walk out smiling, wondering what the heck had her so excited about what Luke is doing for me this year. I push the thought aside and get to work for I'm scared of getting yelled at by Luke. He's very inspired by Cooper's story, which is posted in front of the Cafe and inside the Cafe almost everywhere. We have open mic nights all the time and talents always happen to pop in on the good nights.

****

I sit down at the bar, tired of the long day of work. We end early today because it is Luke and I's anniversary. We celebrate with the family first before we celebrate by ourselves.

"Happy Anniversary," is what the last person in the cafe says before leaving. Now it is just Luke and I. Katherine and I had set up a small little date in the corner booth because I have wanted to show Luke everything, share with him everything. He actually wants to listen.

"Luke, you can come out now." I call him from the back. I stand next to the table, smiling as I watch his face light up from the candles or me, probably me. He moves closer and plants a kiss on my lips, lingering for a while.

"Okay, sit down before the food that I made gets cold." I grin while sitting down. I haven't cooked food in a while due to the fact that Katherine is an amazing cook. I only, rarely, make the food in the house now that Katherine has been educated in the culinary arts. Although, Johnny can make a pretty great Chicken Parmesan, thanks to me.

"It's so good." Luke says, stuffing his mouth with my cooking. He seems so hungry. He rushes through his meal and doesn't hesitate to eat everything on his plate.

"Baby, are you okay? You ate that really quickly." I say, with a worried expression on my face. He was either rushing this or he was really hungry.

"I'm fine. I'm just really hungry." He says, holding his stomach.

"Do you want mine? I can make some more." I say, getting up.

"No," He rushes, "No. I'm fine. I'm actually stuffed now."

"Tell me the whole story. I want to know every juicy detail about Cooper." He smiles at me. It is our anniversary and Luke wants to know everything about another man.

"Luke, it's fine. We don't have to talk about this tonight. We don't have to rush this conversation. It's a pretty big one and it's our anniversary. I don't want to—well, it's about us tonight. Not Cooper." I wipe my mouth with discomfort.

"Cooper is a big part of how you and I got back together. Of course I want to know about the guy who led me to you. I better be sure to thank him when I get up there." I smile at my boyfriend, Lucas James Kelly, the boyfriend that I never thought I would get back. But I did.

Lucas's empty plate tips over from a sudden motion of his hand. It felt as if I couldn't get close enough to outstretch my hand to save the plate from crashing or to get to him to take my hand. The crash came more of like a booming sound instead of the light, delicate

shattering that had been expected. But I would find that

to be the sound that would haunt me for the next couple

of days; the ringing never leaving my vacant mind. I could

hear Lucas calling out my name, as if he was trying to pull

me back into a dimension that I later found out, never

existed at all. Blind spots hindered my vision until all I

saw was black; this when my eyelids lurched open and my

heartbeat skyrocketed.

****

CHAPTER 8:

The first thing I saw when my eyes finally lurched open was a blonde-haired surprised boy, who I had just been having dinner with. But we weren't sitting across from each other, smiling at Table 4, celebrating our anniversary anymore; monitors beeped behind me proving that. I look up at Lucas, dazed and confused, but it seems as if he didn't have all the answers either.

It took me a minute for my brain to form the words I have been wanting to scream since I woke.

"What happened? How did we get here? We were just having dinner in Billy's Bar and now—" I stop myself mid-sentence because Lucas's eyes are telling me something is wrong.

"What is it?"

"Lorraine, you don't remember what happened?" He folds

his hands into his pockets and moves closer to the hospital bed that I had seen so much of in my memories, that I thought to be true.

"The last thing I remember was that we were together, having dinner in Billy's Bar. But from the look on your face," I didn't care if the memories didn't happen. I didn't care if my father was dead, and Linda was fake, and everything I had conjured up in my mind went to shit; the one question that plagued my mind was about one teenage boy and his green eyes.

"It didn't actually happen, did it?" Overwhelming tears spilled on my cheeks like a little school girl; who was I to cry? But the only thing I wanted to know was if he was real, if Cooper was real.

He shakes his head and confirms my worst fears. Did this mean he wasn't real? Did this mean I had just imagined the perfect guy and now he was completely wiped from existence; the existence I would give anything to go back to? But why would I ever want to go back? He was gone and I couldn't change anything about that.

The racing of my mind and emotions finally slowed down when the doctor walked into the room, staring at the bland sheets of paper before he did a double-take at me; he smiles with his eyes because I was awake.

"Lorraine! You're awake. How are you feeling?" The doctor shuffles the papers around and walks to my bedside. His thick glasses threw me off; his eyes seemed so vibrant and bulging but it wasn't very welcoming.

"I feel okay." I fold my arms across my chest and glance down at myself; was I okay? My leg seemed fine though it was resting on a pillow, propped up.

"You had a dislocated arm, a broken leg, and head trauma, which caused the coma. Do you remember what happened to you?" Coma? Had it really been a coma?

"Is this real? You're real?" I point at Lucas, hoping that this wasn't like the alternate reality I had been in. But, of course they would tell me this is real; how could they not? Maybe they thought this was real too.

Lucas nods with odd side glances to the doctor. Was it strange to ask such a simple question? The doctor writes something down and makes me shake with anxiety.

The next two days consisted of scans, as if I was an animal being tested, because not only was it to be sure I was okay, medically, they wanted to make sure I didn't have permanent damage from the coma. After assuring the hospital's provided shrink that I was okay and understood that all that happened was only a dream, they released me after two weeks.

It took me a little while getting used to living in a stranger's apartment but I felt as if I knew Niko because of the dream that I had. He had taken in my brother when my mother checked into the rehabilitation center once again, which I knew to be true because Niko told me.

Johnny being so happy and calm around Niko also made it feel like home.

After a couple of days of staying at the cozy apartment, a man knocked on the door and Niko opened it, allowing him access. His light green eyes struck me from the second I saw him and it was as if the dream had been true but I had to remind myself, it wasn't real once again. His familiarity hit me like the truck that had hit me, causing the coma, which resulted in all the pain I'm feeling right now.

He beckons me with my name, as if he knows me but I wasn't sure if we had ever met before. Sitting down next to me, he puts his hand on mine, as if reassurance could draw me out of my shaking state.

Does this mean Cooper was real after all? Or was he just what my mind has been longing for, ever since I was little and would watch *"I Love Lucy,"* but I was too afraid to question his existence.

"You probably don't know who I am, but my name is Russ and I'm Niko's step-dad. I'm so glad to see that you are awake and okay." I remember sitting on the roof and touching Russell's face but now that seemed too distant. It seemed as though it happened years ago. Yet, I was so close to him that I could make out the etched in lines on his face, ones that Cooper had too, but Cooper wasn't real. Cooper wasn't real.

I had to keep repeating that line during Russell's entire visit. I barely heard a word he said. I couldn't stop staring into his eyes. Those same eyes danced with me in Billy's Bar and saved my life in the alleyway. Now, my own eyes shed tears for the brown-haired boy who taught me that I can save myself by saving others.

A hand touched my knee, which snapped me out of my inner thoughts.

"Lorraine, are you okay? You seem a bit out of it?"

"Yeah I'm okay. Just trying to adjust to all of this." His eyes dart across the room, as if he is looking for ways in which he can bring me out of this funk I had fallen into.

"I know just the place," His abruptness comes as a shock to me and brings multiple dreams back when he smiles at me, mischievously.

"And you could bring your laptop, because I heard from your mother how much you liked to write." I was hesitant at first, afraid what could happen if I took a wrong step. Could I go with him to this place that he had in mind? Did I trust him enough for that yet? I stare into the deep lines in his face and the amount of memories that were made but weren't exactly real. They felt real in the pit of my stomach, and to me, that's all that really counts. I don't care that they were all just a part of my imagination and I sure as hell don't care that a shrink, who hadn't been inside my head, decided they were fake. Just let me live my life.

"Alright, I'll go. Where are we even going?" He smiles wide at the question, as if this place we are going to has a special spot in his heart.

"It's called *Billy's Bar.* I own it. It's a nice little place where you can make some good memories. I have a feeling that you will love it."

For the first time in what feels like long time, I am actually excited about something. The mystery and the fact that I don't know what this place could hold for me scares me, but Cooper taught me to take risks. Even if he wasn't real, that life lesson is still a very important one.

As we get out of the car and I stand in front of Billy's Bar, déjà vu swirling in the leaves beside me. I cross my arms and hold on tight to my jacket, the fall weather bringing chills to my toes.

"Thanks, C!" Russ winks at a man walking into the alleyway, with a big black garage bag and for a second, I think I see Cooper. But it can't be him; he's not real. I convinced myself he hadn't been because where would he even be now? Even if he was, according to my dreams, he would be dead. There was no hope, no matter how much was tucked into my middle name.

Russ keeps a soft hand on my back and we stroll into the bar doors together, the clinging bringing back so many emotions. Tears fiercely swim in the deep rough waters of my eyes and debate falling but I won't let them. I give Russ a smile before taking my laptop in my stride, under my arm, and walking to the corner booth with confidence.

It looks and feels exactly the same as the last time I had been in it but part of it feels different and I know part of it feels different because I had never been in the corner booth. Until now, of course. The cushion feels as delicate as it feels before but somehow different; he isn't there.

I open my laptop and begin typing from the first thing I remember after the crash. Maybe if I write my memories as a fictitious novel, it will feel less real to me. I hope I can finally get closure and move on with my life.

As I finish my first page of the novel, I hear voices coming from the bar. I look up and see Russell standing next to a girl wearing an apron, with brown hair just like mine. They were laughing with one another, Russell's eyes gleaming as she finally opened a beer bottle and the popping sound echoed through my ears. I don't realize the tears have finally won the war and slip down my face until they hit the letter C on my keyboard.

This was too overwhelming for myself to handle. I think I have to leave. But as I try to shift my body weight up, my legs feel like putty and I can't stand. It takes me a few minutes to regroup and once I do, I begin typing again. After I finish page two, I hear noises from the bar again. Only this time it isn't voices; it is movements. I know not to look up again because it will only remind me of that green-eyed boy and his dazzling smile, so I keep my head down with all of my might and continue to type.

Suddenly, I hear footsteps coming towards me. I have no choice this time. I have to look up. My gaze meets a familiar hand that is holding a mug containing what looks to be my latte. My eyes shift to the side, using my peripheral vision and I see the apron that I saw only moments before. It's only Russell I assure myself. There is no need to even look up. A moment passes and who I think to be Russell, still hasn't walked away. I feel his stare burning through my skin and the fire ignites red in my cheeks. But when I look up, the redness in my cheeks quickly gets extinguishes and it looks as if I've just seen a ghost, and I have.

It's him. It's finally him. The question that has been on replay in my head since I woke up had awaited an answer and now the answer is staring me in the face. The second his green eyes temptingly lock on mine, my mouth goes dry and words become distant, as if I wasn't just typing away on my computer. He draws the peace and acceptance out of my system and replaces it with reality.

We look at each other for what seems like forever until he speaks up.

"We never formally met before but I'm Russell's son. My name is Cooper. I've heard a lot about you. It's great to see that you are awake. How are you doing? I mean—are you okay?" He itches the back of his neck like I remember he did when he was extremely uncomfortable.

"I'm better now." Not only was I better because I was awake and conscious but also because Cooper was there.

"I'm so happy to see you awake." I can't help but blush when I recall our kiss in my memory. How could I act as if we've never met before?

"How'd you know?" I point at the mug before wrapping my hand around it and taking a sip. Two sugars. How did he know?

"I was in the hospital for a night and I was talking to your mom before she went into rehabilitation. She couldn't stop talking about you, even told me your favorite type of coffee as if you were this angel from Heaven and I just knew I had to meet you one day. Something about your eyes just seems so *familiar*." He slides into the opposite seat and points to the picture frame above my head.

"Did you notice the drawing?" My stomach started churning as my neck turned and my eyes collided with a photo of me, one in which Cooper drew.

"I saw you that night and I knew one day, you would be here, sitting in this corner booth. Your mom told me you loved to write and I figured you'd be typing away with your latte. The image just looked so beautiful in my head, I had to draw it out and share it with the world. I just realized how creepy that sounds. I'm sorry." He shakes his head with laughter echoing through the booth but not only from him, from me as well. The drawing was just as I remember it. This image of someone who I didn't know was me. How could I be this beautiful god-send that he was talking about? How could he see me so gracefully through his golf-course-green eyes.

"It's not creepy at all." The stereo in the background becomes more prominently heard because a familiar song came whispering through the speakers. *"Please Don't Go,"* starts shocking my stomach and makes me gape because how more perfect of a moment could it play? Sitting here beside a real Cooper, playing one of our real songs, with a *real* romance blossoming. It couldn't become more immaculate. My jaw drops and Cooper sees the familiarity in my face.

"You know this song? It's one of my favorites." He grins widely, leaning back on the booth with one shoulder, making him appeal to me so much more.

"I have the craziest story to tell you. If you'd like to listen to it, that is." His smile tells me to continue, like it had in my dream sequence. His green eyes connect with mine and bring my heart out to sing a story of love and passion.

Our glistening eyes were the looking glasses into the future and through mine, he could tell that we would be stuck in the corner booth, holding onto our songs, enchanted at the drawing, and writing little blog posts about ourselves for the rest of our lives; happy yet knowing the consequences of time. Time is a valuable thing.

****

EPILOGUE:

It seemed as if after we locked eyes, we knew nothing would be the same. My story intrigued him because according to him, he would have made the same exact choices my "dream" Cooper would've made, which didn't make him much of a dream anymore. I didn't know where to draw the line of reality but that would take me several years to accomplish; even so, it became negligible to me to achieve.

Having all these coma "memories" founded my life in ways that I cannot imagine waking up without. My mother had gone to rehab and I had processed that in my own way during my coma, along with my father truly going to jail for murder, but he didn't kill Cooper; he killed Dr. Nova. When I went to visit him, my father told me how she was the easiest one to get to. I left him after that and have promised myself to never see him again. Though I didn't know her in reality, I still showed my deepest empathy to Niko and even visited Linda's grave, who had lost her life to suicide, just like I had seen in my visions of reality.

Eventually, my story got told on pages and the eyes of my loved ones would be plagued with my coma memories. Cooper would end up being the most enchanted by them, him taking them to be published by a famous publishing house of some sorts. My alternate reality would never compare to the reality that I had started to live when I met Cooper and continue to know him, for the rest of my life.

Our story didn't end at the hand of a knife or at the crash of a vehicle, causing a coma. Our story would flash by us and one year later, we would be in the same places. Cooper was enrolled in college, paid in full because of his art scholarship. But it was my turn and since we had never gone on that road trip, we decided it was better late than never to go look at colleges like I had planned with him during my coma.

A honk is heard from the cracked-open window in my room and as I finish my makeup, I smile, knowing it is the brown-haired boy with his emerald green eyes. Grabbing my purse, I lock the door hurriedly and run down the stairs, almost losing my balance but the banister backs me up. I cannot hide my excitement to see Cooper Allen Ross, my boyfriend. His beaten-up Cadillac idles in the middle of the street, blocking a couple of cars with infuriated people behind the wheels of them. Their expressions cannot change mine as I run out of the apartment building and into the passenger seat of his beautiful red car.

"Hi, honey." I lean over the gearshift and clutch the stubs of brown hair on his lower neck, pecking his lips with mine as if it was the simplest action that didn't cause a supernova in the pit of my stomach. The honking behind us starts but Cooper proceeds to flick down his Ray Band shades he spent the whole winter saving up for. With one hand on the wheel and the other resting against my mid-thigh, he speeds off towards the bar in style, as if it isn't only a couple of minutes away.

"You excited?" He glances over at my loss of bags but reassurance floods out through my hand laying against his on my thigh. I nod, bringing his hand up to where his knuckles met my lips. He takes his fingers and runs them down my cheek, his eyes darting over to mine.

"Keep your eyes on the road, Coop. You don't want a repeat coma." I joke, holding his hand close to my chest as his eyes refocus back on the road, knowing another coma would not put us in the green.

"You can't do things to my hand like that and expect me not to be mesmerized by you, Lo." He takes the hand that had once been in mine and holds the back of my neck, pushing his lips against my cheekbone with care and with force, but at the same time, it seems delicate and appreciated.

"Coop! Come on, the road!" The car swerves a little as we are cruising down the small streets to get to the busy ones.

"Ass." I mutter, rolling my eyes as a smile erupts on my face as soon as I utter the words. My thoughts and my smiles had Cooper's name all over them.

"What was that, potty mouth?" He hits my shoulder, playfully and soft, grabbing my side and tickling me with his extra muscles that he gained during the winter as well.

"Cooper, stop!" I chuckle, shoving his hand away as my skirt drew farther up my thighs than originally supposed to. He stops right when my skirt was practically up my legs and I slap him for it, shaking my head as I pull it down.

"Even in my coma, you still found ways of seeing too much of me." I laugh, looking out the window, remembering the dance in the bar and wanting that scene to be real. His hand lands on my left thigh again, covered by my red flare skirt, matching his car.

"Will you tell me what you want to study already? I've been waiting anxiously." Last night, I had decided what career I wanted to follow and ever since then, I shut Cooper out on his all-powerful knowledge about me. He had many guesses on the phone last night but I wouldn't give anything away. I wanted to announce it before we left on the best and only road trip of my life.

"Like I told you on the phone last night, Coop. My lips are sealed until we get to the bar." In reality, I just wanted it to be a surprise for Cooper because though we were going on a road trip to thousands of different colleges all over, I knew I wasn't going to anywhere fancy. New York always held my heart and that wasn't going to change.

"The things you do to me, Lorraine. Lucky I love you." He rolls his eyes and pulls into the small alleyway that we decided to turn into a parking spot for Cooper. I can't help but grab his hand as soon as he rounds the car towards the entrance of Billy's Bar and stroll with him towards new beginnings.

"Surprise!" Everyone screamed as Cooper cracked out the door and he switched the lights on. My mom, Russell, Johnny, and Niko stand around the bar, shooting out from different spots. Balloon floating around and magic in my eyes, I felt it wasn't a surprise until I said to Cooper what I needed to.

"You told me once that I had to do something special with my life because I owed it to myself and to you and to everyone who wasn't destined for greatness in the world. So I decided instead of taking the stereotypical path you would have excepted me to take, I'm going to become a doctor. I'm going to study and go into med school and figure out what I want to specialize in but I'm going to make you proud and also study English on the side because that's my number one passion. But I *want* to go into the med industry and help people. I want to be the reason some parent gets to—" Cooper's arms encircle my body and he twirls me around in the air, laughing along with me.

"That's amazing, Lorraine! I'm so proud of you." He lets me grab the floor again and scoops my cheeks in his warm palms, bringing his lips softly on mine.

"Lorraine! Tell him the rest!" Johnny chuckles from behind the corner of the bar as he jumps up and down just to see me and Coop.

"Okay, John." I laugh, shaking my head side to side before looking into Cooper's eyes and seeing the same dashing smile that I had grown to love more than any other. "I decided on where I am going to college. I didn't need the road trip to figure out that I belong here at the bar and with you. So I'm going to school at NYU and I'm going to be able to come work here all the time because I can drive back and forth. And since you are going to FIT, I can come and meet up and we could get lunch some days, if that's what you would-"

His lips crash against mine in a desperate attempt to make me love him more. It seems as if I really got to live our kiss scene more than once and I am very grateful for that. He doesn't stop kissing me but moves to wrap his arms around my waist, pushing me the tightest he can to press up against him but due to Cooper's straining height, he has to make due. Clapping from those who mean the most comes dashing into our ears and I know for the rest of our lives, it's going to be this joyful because we are together. Everything for, at least, the bulk of our lives is going to be okay because he's there. He's breathing and he wants to be mine.

"Cooper, can we eat now?" Johnny smiles up at my boyfriend as he pulls on the hem of his shirt, clearly satisfied now that the surprise had been shed.

"Sure, bud. But we didn't-" Cooper doesn't realize that I planned all this yet.

"It's a road trip party. I thought of food too, don't worry." He kisses my forehead and wraps his arm around my shoulders, amazement shining in his eyes for me.

"Everyone gather around the table. I'm starving." I sigh, sitting myself next to Cooper and Johnny, my two favorite boys.

"Hey, I heard that." A slightly angered Niko huffs, as I hadn't realized that I had said my two favorite boys aloud.

"Don't worry, Niko. You are secretly my favorite." He winks at me before a hand slides onto my thigh and squeezes, teasing me.

Oh, Coop. Jealousy never did look good on you. I grasp his hand and lock our fingers together, reassuring him. I lean into his shoulder and tuck a falling hair behind my ear. Cooper's arm wraps around my shoulders and holds my right shoulder in his grasp.

All of us fit into the corner booth and I am lucky enough to sit on the side where I can make out the view of the drawing of myself. My heart will stay in that leather-cushioned corner booth for the rest of my life.

Footsteps can be heard from inside the kitchen which made me suspicious because we were all sitting around the table. Who could be in the kitchen?

The door shoots open and out darts Katherine, holding plates loaded with food as if she was serving people.

"Katherine! What are you-" Lucas comes out of the doors as well, holding onto more plates.

"What is-"

"Eat up guys." She sets down each of our plates and inside is chicken parmesan. Johnny's favorite.

"Aww, awesome! My favorite!" Johnny takes his fork and gets to work on cleaning his plate.

Katherine couldn't cook but she wanted to and a culinary school in the city was delighted to have her. She would be a chef here in the bar while she learned and even after, I'm sure she would find a home here. She brightly grins at me, Luke placing the plates on the table and sliding his arm, protectively around Katherine as he did.

At the motion, her eyes shoot up at mine but with understanding, I shoot them down. Though a shocker, I am not bothered by their relationship. I have my own relationship to savor. His hand hangs off my shoulder and his eyes bore into mine with desire and hope for the future. My smile assures the green-eyed boy that our future would be dazzling than the sun and more sparkling than the stars.

As everyone eats their chicken, my stomach turns and I hold my knee, beckoning for it to stop. But I realize that my stomach pangs for a reason when I glance up from my plate and see Luke's hands, covered in red splotches.

"What happened to your hands?" Such a compelling question for me but a dull question for him, he answers without confusion.

"I burned them trying to make the chicken." He chuckles, his eyes darting down to glare at the red burns covering his fingers.

"He knew the recipe by heart though. It was very strange." Katherine leans into Luke as they carry their own plates from the kitchen and squeeze into the spacious corner booth. We feel like a real family.

The fact that Luke burned his hands on the chicken recipe and knew it by heart brought chaos to my mind. Where do I draw the line to reality and dreaming?

But I glance beside me and all that built-up anguish and pain washes away. I have Cooper. And he would be there always to draw the line between what matters and what doesn't.

THE END.

ACKNOWLEDGEMENTS:

I'd like to thank God for making all of this truly possible. I'm so thankful for everything He has given me.

As I continue to step forward in life, I will always carry this story with me. As I continue to grow and prosper, I will reflect and try to realize how completely blessed I am to have this life with amazing people, amazing accomplishments, and amazing stories that I can still write.

I'd like to thank my family; my father, mother, Alexis, Will, Duke, Jax, and Cooper for making this possible. I love you guys with all my heart. Alexis, thank you for helping me make the cover.

I'd like to thank my best friend, who has always pushed me to live this dream out and who has always wanted me to have better things; this is the better that I've always wanted. Mads, I love you. Thank you for your unconditional support.

I'd especially like to thank Kris, for helping me through the editing process of this book and being there for me whenever I need. Thanks for putting up with my annoying self.

I'd like to thank my teachers, especially my English teachers who over the years, have encouraged my writing and helped me grow. A special thanks to Mr. Hafker for giving me advice on the process and for helping me develop my writing style.

And I'd like to thank everyone who has gone through any type of struggle in their life, for hanging on enough to see the glistening, bright landscape, after a pitch-black night.

****

Made in the USA
Middletown, DE
20 April 2018